Z   d her with his piercing blue eyes. He'd never really looked at her so
i   re, and that made Jade even more nervous. "I think that would be very
c   d, tucking a strand of hair behind one ear. "I like the harmony we put
c   e of the song. Can Charlie sing that with you?"

"   " Zephyr said as he ordered a can of Red Bull and a bottle of water. "If
r   you can sit in with us."

"   enaline shot through Jade's body as she thought of performing onstage
v   r and Side Effects. She'd dreamed about this moment! "I'd love it!" she
fi   ed out.

Z   touched her elbow with his hand. "Cool. I'll see you on the ice."

Read more

Love Letters:

Perfect Strangers

Love Letters:

mixed messages

JAHNNa N. mALCoLm

SIMON AND SCHUSTER

SIMON AND SCHUSTER

First published in Great Britain in 2006 by Simon & Schuster UK Ltd
Africa House, 64-78 Kingsway, London WC2B 6AH
A Viacom company.

Originally published in 2005 by Simon Pulse,
an imprint of Simon & Schuster Children's Division, New York.

Text copyright © 2005 by Jahnna Beecham and Malcolm Hillgartner
Cover illustration © 2005 Jerry Paris
Cover design by Tracey Hurst

A CIP catalogue record for this book is available from the British Library.

ISBN: 1-416-91048-4

1 3 5 7 9 10 8 6 4 2

Printed and bound in Great Britain by
Bookmarque Ltd, Croydon, Surrey

1

"Truth or Dare!" Jade Chandler announced as she reached the top of Signature Hill.

Her best friends, Keesha Kelly and Lucy Mercer, were behind her, still climbing up the grassy slope. Below them lay the rectangular buildings of Wheaton High School. Off in the distance, the glass windows on the downtown buildings of Cincinnati glowed in the early light.

"What are we, like *ten*?" Keesha struggled to keep her super-straightened, highly glued, jet-black hair from blowing everywhere in the stiff breeze coming off the Ohio River. "Plus, it's seven in the morning."

"And the first day of school," Lucy said,

holding up the hem of her vintage dress to keep from tripping over it. "The first day of our last year of high school."

"Exactly!" Jade shouted into the wind. "Could there be a more perfect time to be truthful or daring?" She threw her arms wide and tossed her head back so her long red hair whipped out behind her like flames.

Keesha and Lucy grinned up at their friend. In her shredded jeans and black tee, Jade looked like some kind of punk scarecrow. Her wrists were dripping with bracelets, and silver chains and beaded necklaces were draped around her neck.

Every year since they were freshmen, on the first day of school, the three friends had climbed to the top of the big white W made of rocks, which was located on Signature Hill, behind Wheaton High and right above the parking lot. It was a perfect place for people watching. Meeting here was Jade's idea, like most things they did. She liked to think of the first day of school the way other people viewed New Year's Day: as a chance to make a fresh start.

"Haven't you forgotten something, O fearless leader girl?" Keesha asked as she took her traditional spot on top of the white rocks that formed the first line in the W.

Jade stood in the center of the W and cocked her head. "Give me a clue."

"The sign-in." Lucy carefully pulled three marking pens from the tiny crocheted bag that hung from her shoulder. She handed one to each of her friends and then knelt down at her place on the last line of the W. "Each year we put our initials and the date on one of these white rocks."

Lucy used a purple marker to write her initials and draw yet another peace sign— she'd drawn one each year of high school— on her rock. Under the date she wrote the word BELIEVE! Lucy's parents were total hippies and very active in the world peace movement. Lucy tried hard to follow in their footsteps.

Keesha wrote her initials in red, of course. As a fashion leader, her clothes, hair, and makeup always reflected the color that was au courant. This month's color was red. Under her initials, Keesha the party girl wrote, ROCK THEIR SOCKS OFF!

Finally, Jade knelt to write her name and date. Each time, she tried to write some inspirational words to carry her through the year. When they were freshmen, she'd written, SPREAD YOUR WINGS AND FLY! and she'd done just that. She hadn't worried about being a member of the popular crowd or fitting in. She dressed the way she wanted and took up the guitar. Now, as she entered her last year of high school and faced so many choices ahead, she wanted a phrase that would give her courage. So Jade wrote, SHOOT THE MOON!

She stood up and turned to her friends. "Okay," Jade said. Then she asked, "Who wants to be first to tell a Truth?"

"So we're gonna do this. I'll go first," Keesha said. "The truth doesn't scare me."

Keesha stood with her hands on the waist of her black suede mini. A gust of wind whipped her ankle-length red cardigan out behind her, nearly pulling her over backward. She steadied herself and then spoke, rocking her head in her sassy Keesha way. "I'm extremely glad we're seniors, because I don't think I could take another couple of years of this broken-down sorry excuse for a school. I just wish I hadn't signed up for Computer Aided Design. I hate that evil troll, Mr. Bedford, and I hate computers."

"So why did you take CAD?" Jade asked.

"Because of Kip Logan," Keesha shot back.

"You chose a class because of a *guy*?" Lucy asked, wide-eyed.

"Kip is not just any guy!" Keesha said, wrapping her sweater around her to shield herself from the wind. "While you and your family were off eating granola in the woods this summer, and while Jade was at that guitar camp, Kip and I became extremely tight. Then at registration in August, Kip was all, 'Let's take as many classes as we can together.' And I'm like, 'Whatever you say, Kip.' And two weeks later, he can't remember my name and I'm stuck in CAD."

Jade laughed. "Serves you right!"

"That is so unlike you," Lucy said in surprise. "I mean, it's *weak*."

Keesha threw her head back and moaned, "I know!"

Jade jabbed her finger at Keesha. "I dare you to go to your counselor's office this morning and tell him you took some random course just for a guy. I'm sure Mr. Boggs will let you switch."

"Not fair!" Lucy protested. "That's an easy dare."

"For you, the hippie girl, maybe," Keesha said. "But for me, who takes orders from no one? I will look like such a loser."

Jade spun to face Lucy. "Your turn. Truth!"

Lucy chewed nervously on her lip and paced to the top of the hill, preparing to make her confession. She looked like the perfect hippie child—tanned and blond, with her curly hair gathered loosely on the top of her head and wrapped with a frayed green linen scarf. A tiny gold nose ring and a crystal on a pink satin necklace were the only jewelry she wore today. She spun back to face them, and her long, flowered skirt curled around her ankles.

"Remember when my family went camping and I said we had a wonderful time? Well, it wasn't because of the mountain air, or the hiking." She looked at Keesha and added, "Or the granola. I met a boy in the Blue Ridge Mountains."

"Aha!" Keesha pointed at Lucy. "Then I'm not alone."

Jade frowned. "Why didn't you tell us?"

"I didn't want you to think I bailed on you guys because I got a boyfriend," Lucy replied, covering her face with one hand. "We always said we'd stay true to ourselves and not let boys run our lives like all the other girls do at Wheaton High."

"So, what's this hunk of love's name?" Keesha teased.

Lucy dropped her hand and smiled. Her pale blue eyes sparkled. "Chris Sutton. He's the coolest guy—really into the outdoors, totally honest, and he goes to Fairmont High, right across town."

"So is this Chris guy a vegetarian?" Jade asked, remembering Lucy's recent vow to never eat meat.

Lucy blinked in surprise. "Of course."

"Well, that's a relief," Keesha cracked. "I'd hate to think you'd sold out and were suddenly eating Big Macs and Chicken McNuggets."

Lucy laughed. "No, we've only gone to the Natural Café or Noodles."

"Whoa!" Jade dropped her arms to her side in surprise. "This is news to me. I talk to you nearly every day on the phone and you've never mentioned him once."

Lucy stared at the ground, embarrassed.

"We've gone out a couple of times," she admitted with a sheepish grin. "I just didn't know how to tell you."

"That's all right, Lucy Goosey. I'm really happy you found a guy who's so right for you," Keesha said as she dug in her bag for her lip gloss. She carefully applied it as she spoke. "I know we all promised we'd be strong, and you'd stay an artist and Jade would remain a musician and I'd do whatever it is I do. But let's face it: It's time for some male attention. And even though Kip Logan turned out to be a total jerk, he's still really smart and hot. And I'm going to stay in my CAD class so that I can let him know how smart and hot I am."

Jade couldn't stand it anymore. She leaped onto the boulder at the very top of Signature Hill and shouted, "Okay! I have a confession to make."

Keesha folded her arms across her chest. "Lay it on us, fearless leader girl."

Jade focused her dark green eyes on Keesha. "For four solid years I have been hopelessly in love with Zephyr Strauss."

"The music man?" Keesha gasped.

"Awesome!" Lucy said, clapping her hands together.

Zephyr Strauss was Wheaton High School's leading rocker. His band, Side Effects, was really starting to make a name for itself in the tristate area.

"He's perfect for you!" Keesha declared.

"I've never done anything about it," Jade said, hopping down off the boulder. "I've only worshipped him from afar."

"So tell me something new," Keesha said, putting one hand on her hip. "I had a crush on him our entire sophomore year."

"For real?" Jade asked.

Keesha nodded, and then Lucy confessed, "And I had one all last year."

"Which isn't so unusual," Keesha added. "Half the girls at Wheaton only go to Side Effects shows to Zephyr-gaze."

"For three years I've known his schedule," Jade continued. "I knew where he'd be at what hour. I made sure I accidentally bumped into him in the hall before lunch. And I would race to be at my locker when he passed by at the end of the day. Isn't that sick?"

"That's dedication." Keesha shook her head in awe.

"And here's the worst of it. . . ." Jade

squeezed her eyes shut. "I even started play-ing the guitar because I thought it might make Zephyr notice me."

"Whoa!" Keesha murmured. "That's seri-ous."

"Isn't that amazing?" Lucy smiled as she looped her arm through Jade's. "You turned into this totally hot musician all because of a little crush."

"'Little'?" Keesha repeated, raising one eyebrow. "More like *humongous*."

"Whatever." Lucy waved one hand at Keesha to quiet her. "The point is, Jade was born to play music, and who cares what made her get started."

"You're not mad at me for holding out on you?" Jade asked. "I'm the one who said friends tell one another everything. I also warned that boys would be our downfall. Clearly, I haven't been listening to my own advice."

"Hey, we're almost out of school," Keesha said with a shrug. "If we can't handle boys now, when *will* we be able to handle them?"

Jade slumped down on the boulder in relief.

Lucy knelt beside her and whispered, "Dare time."

Keesha agreed. "I think we should dare Jade to tell Zephyr she loves him."

"That's good," Lucy giggled excitedly. "Jade should call him and tell him how she feels."

Jade nearly choked. "Never! What if he hangs up or says something really rude? I couldn't handle the humiliation."

Keesha shrugged. "Then write him."

Jade rolled her eyes. "That is *so* junior high."

Keesha put her hands on her hips and waggled her head back and forth. "It worked in junior high, and it'll work now. But, hey, if you just want to spend your senior year obsessing over Zephyr Strauss, then that is your choice."

"I am not obsessing over Zephyr Strauss!" Jade shouted just as Zephyr's red Toyota 4Runner pulled into the parking lot. Some students who had gathered to talk by their cars heard Jade shout and looked up at the hill.

Jade covered her mouth with her hand. "Did Courtney and Caitlin hear that?" she whispered.

Courtney Kass and Caitlin Winters were two major gossips at Wheaton High.

Keesha was laughing so hard, she was snorting. "Maybe you don't have to make a call or write a letter after all. Courtney and Caitlin will deliver the message for you."

Jade put her hand over Keesha's mouth. "It's not funny. They'll tell Zephyr, and I'll be humiliated."

"Oh, don't be so dramatic," Keesha yelled as she brushed Jade's hand away. "Wouldn't be the worst thing in the world if Zeph found out you were hot for him."

"Speaking of humiliation," Lucy cut in, "I don't think it's a good idea to be late on the first day of school."

"You're right," Jade said, straightening up. "The last thing I need is some annoying teacher on my back. . . . I have enough things to worry about."

As they neared the parking lot, which had become crowded with cars and students, Jade bent over to catch her breath. "Now remember," she huffed to her friends, "what we said on the hill stays on the hill."

Lucy nodded toward Jade. "I won't tell."

"Me neither," Keesha vowed. A mischievous smile crept across her face as she added, "But you may want to. Look who's coming up the sidewalk—*right behind you.*" She spoke the last three words in an exaggerated whisper.

Jade's eyes widened into two huge green circles. She didn't dare look. "I'm going inside," she said stiffly. "School's about to start."

Keesha caught her by the arm. "Now hold on. Don't you want to say hey to Zephyr?" Keesha wiggled her eyebrows. "It would be a perfect time to mention the *enormous* crush you have on him."

Jade glanced nervously over her shoulder. Zephyr was walking with Charlie Riddle, the bass player in his band. Zephyr was looking more and more like a rock star with every passing minute. His bleached blond hair was spiked out over his forehead. He wore a well-worn leather jacket over a Fox Motocross tee, and vertical-striped jeans. Silver chains hung from his belt, and a leather bracelet with silver studs was strapped around his wrist. Zephyr could never be called cute; he was ruggedly handsome.

"I don't want to talk to Zephyr," Jade hissed to Keesha. "And if you mention 'enormous crush' one more time, I will probably have to kill you."

"That's extreme," Keesha muttered as she followed Jade up to the front door of the school.

Lucy trotted along beside them. "Keesha's only trying to help."

"Yeah, right." Jade flung the door open with so much force that it slammed into the back of a boy chatting with a teacher outside the front entrance. He turned in surprise.

"Sorry, Adam." Jade winced in embarrassment. "I didn't see you there."

Adam Lockhart was wearing his usual outfit: plain white shirt, narrow black tie, black khakis, and an old-fashioned derby. When he saw Jade he gave her a warm smile. "No problem, Jade," he said, tipping the brim of his derby. "Didn't need that back, anyway."

Jade returned his smile and was about to say more, when Keesha shoved her through the doorsill into the hallway.

"What's with that Adam boy?" Keesha whispered as they made their way down the hall to their lockers. "He could be a cute guy if he wanted to. But he dresses like some kind of thrift shop refugee. Plus, he drives that soccer-mom minivan."

"Maybe he's a Mormon missionary," Lucy suggested.

"No!" Keesha waved a hand. "Those guys ride bikes. And they definitely don't wear funky hats."

Jade had pushed ahead, anxious to avoid running into Zephyr, when she was stopped by Kara LaCross, a fellow songwriter and musician. "Jade! I caught your set at Evo's open mike last Monday," Kara said. "I like your sound."

"Thanks, Kara. They asked me to come back next weekend," Jade said. She would have liked to tell Kara about the new song she was trying to write, and the sparkle-red Fender Telecaster Custom guitar she'd just bought. But Keesha and Lucy wouldn't let her—they were on a mission.

Keesha pulled Jade to the side-by-side lockers that they'd had since freshman year. "Zephyr is coming down the hall right now. If you don't address this enor"—she put her hand over her mouth and corrected herself—"*regular*-size crush, then you may be doomed to spend your very last year in high school pining away alone."

Jade held up one hand. "Okay, Keesha, you win! I will write a letter to Zephyr declaring my undying passion for him. I will tell him that I can't live another day without him. And I will beg him to be mine. Forever and ever."

Keesha didn't speak for a long time. Finally she said, "That's a start."

Lucy hopped up and down. "Can I deliver the letter?"

Jade rolled her eyes. "Whatever."

Luckily for Jade the buzzer sounded, signaling the start of another school year. She fell back against her locker in relief.

2

Three classes, one lunch, and an assembly later, Jade checked her schedule. Music Theory with Cleavon Cooper. "All right," she murmured. "Now it's time for some fun."

Her other classes—American Poetry, European History, and French 3—were all fine, but this was the class she'd fought hard to get.

Mr. C, as everyone at school called him, had been voted favorite teacher at Wheaton High for five years in a row. Cleavon Cooper had turned the school's forgettable marching band into an award-winner by adding funk to their sound and cool moves to their choreography. When it came to music, Mr. C was like an encyclopedia: He seemed to know about everything musical for the last four centuries. Going to his classes was like sitting in on a freewheeling jam session hosted by Mozart, Duke Ellington, and Tupac all rolled into one.

Jade threw open the door to the music room and froze. Mr. C was seated at the grand piano in the center of the room, noodling through a complex series of jazz chords. With his shaved head and owlish sunglasses, he looked like an aging P. Diddy. Sitting across from him in the front row of folding chairs was only one student—Zephyr Strauss. Jade was already backing out of the room when Mr. C spotted her.

"Jade!" Mr. C called with a big smile. "Get yourself down here, and let's make a little music."

Jade was mystified. Usually every chair in Mr. C's class was filled with a student. "Where is everybody?" she asked, still hesitating at the top of the stairs.

Mr. C waved one hand. "Big mix-up with the schedule. My second period had seventy-five kids. It was kickin'. They were sharing chairs, lying on the floor, swinging from the rafters," he said with a throaty chuckle. "But that's going to change. So, for today only, it's just you, me, and the Zeph-Man."

Zephyr nodded up at Jade and mumbled, "Hey."

One word from Zephyr was enough to make her cheeks blaze a bright pink. That had never happened before. She wondered if all that talk about boys that morning had turned her into some kind of blushing freak. Jade put her head down and trotted down the stairs to the front row of chairs.

Mr. C got up from the piano and went to one of the instrument lockers lining the back of the music room. He pulled out two acoustic guitars and handed one to each of them. "I know this class is Music Theory, but we can't really get down to business until the schedule gets straightened out. So what do you say we play today?"

Suddenly Jade was nervous. She and Zephyr had shared a few music classes before, but she'd never actually jammed with him. As for Zephyr, he seemed totally comfortable with the idea. The second he was handed his guitar, he ran through the power chord introduction to his band's signature tune, "Big Trouble Ahead."

Mr. C slipped behind the piano and added a thumping bass line. Jade let Zephyr play through the song once so she could hear the chord progression. Then she joined in. Mr. C and Zephyr traded solos back and forth while Jade kept a solid rhythm going underneath. When they finished, Zephyr actually smiled at Jade and said, "Nice work."

Jade blushed with pleasure. Then Mr. C shocked her by asking, "So, Jade, got anything to play for us?"

"Well, um, I-I've been working on a new song," she stammered. "I call it 'Shoot the Moon,' but it's not finished."

"That's okay," Mr. C encouraged. "Go on, give us a little sample."

Jade swallowed hard and tried to forget that Zephyr Strauss was sitting just three feet away from her, listening to her song. She played through the introduction and a verse of the song, then stopped. "That's all I have. Sorry."

When she looked up, she caught Zephyr and Mr. C exchanging glances of approval. Then Zeph turned to her and said slowly,

"That . . . was . . . simply . . . beautiful."

"Umm," Mr. C agreed. "Jade, I want to hear that again when you get it finished. And that's an assignment."

Of course, this sent another blast of flaming color into her cheeks.

Then Mr. C pulled some flyers off a stack piled on the piano. "Zeph, you already know about the Battle of the Bands coming up, but pass a few of these entry forms out to your musician friends, will you?" Mr. C handed them to Zephyr, adding with a grin, "We need to drum up a little competition this year for you boys."

Zephyr chuckled. Side Effects had won the Battle of the Bands two years running. Most people considered them a shoo-in to win again.

"I'll do it this Saturday," Zephyr said. "We've got a gig at the Atomic Café. Lots of local players will be there."

"Excellent," Mr. C said. Then he surprised Jade by handing her one of the yellow flyers. "You take one of these, too, Jade. Work up that song you just did and try out."

"Me?" Jade was flattered. "Oh, I don't know. . . ."

"Hey, no need for audition anxiety," Mr. C reassured her. "The auditions are by demo only. No pressure. Put something down on tape or CD and run it by the entry committee. You won't even need to be in the room."

"But I'm a solo act," Jade protested. "Do they take those?"

"Sure," Zephyr said, fixing her with a steady gaze.

"Now, there's no guarantee you'll get a spot on the program," Mr. C cautioned. Then his eyes twinkled as he added, "But as chairperson of the entry committee, I *can* guarantee that your entry will receive careful consideration." Jade still hesitated, and Mr. C added, "You'll never have a chance to win if you don't enter."

"Mr. C's right," Zephyr agreed. "Give it a go."

"Thanks, Zephyr," Jade said, trying to smile casually. "Maybe I will." She carefully folded the flyer in half and tucked it into the back pocket of her jeans. As she did, Jade noticed that Zephyr seemed to be watching her every move. Maybe he was interested in her too?

Mr. C led them both in another piece.

This one was the Peter Gabriel classic "In Your Eyes." Jade knew the words by heart because she'd seen the old movie *Say Anything* at least a dozen times. At the chorus, Zeph added a vocal harmony and they sang together: "In your eyes, the light, the heat, in your eyes, I am complete." Jade was struck by how well their voices blended.

They finished seconds before the end of the period.

"Umm, that was tasty," Mr. C purred. "You two got a good thing going there vocally."

Jade look at Zephyr, who grinned. "Not bad," he agreed, nodding his head.

As they were leaving the classroom, Mr. C said, "Too bad we can't keep our class this small. I really enjoyed it."

"Me too," Zephyr said, turning to give Jade another admiring look. "Catch you tomorrow."

Jade waved good-bye too. She fumbled with putting her books away, to create an excuse to stay behind. The second Mr. C and Zephyr left the classroom, she jumped up and down, squealing with excitement.

After a minute Jade regained her cool

and stepped out into the mob of students heading for their lockers at the end of the day. Could there have been a better first day of school? She didn't think so.

That night, Jade went out to her garage studio to do her homework and work on her audition tape for the Battle of the Bands. She couldn't stop thinking about Zephyr, and Keesha and Lucy's dare. In fact, she knew she'd never get anything done until she wrote her love letter to Zephyr. But how to begin?

Should she be poetic? *My heart flies up when I see you.* No, too sappy.

How about straightforward sincere? *I like you. A lot. Do you like me?* Way too forward and too sincere.

Casual? *A funny thing happened to me on the way to my senior year . . . I fell for you.* Better.

Jade practiced writing her letter on fancy paper in the lavender-colored ink that she always used to write her songs. She decided that made it look too studied. She wanted her note to look laid-back, like something dashed off on a sheet of notebook paper with a ballpoint pen.

Jade crossed to the garage door and shouted

into the house, "Does anyone have a regular old pen?"

Her mother was at her desk in the kitchen. On the phone, of course. As a single mom, Kit Chandler worked round the clock on her real estate deals. Jade's older brother, Nick, who was in his second year at the University of Cincinnati, had taken over their tiny front living room with his stacks of books and papers. Nick was sitting on the couch hunched over a sociology textbook, listening to his iPod on a set of earbud headphones. He was totally oblivious to Jade's attempts to get his attention.

She moved down the hall to the bedroom she shared with her fifteen-year-old sister. As usual, April was at her desk studying. She was an uptight organization freak who put little white printed labels on everything. Jade had given April the labeler for her thirteenth birthday and had regretted it ever since.

One side of their bedroom—Jade's side—looked like a normal teenager's room. She had lots of posters of rock bands on the wall, plus a floor-to-ceiling bulletin board papered with funny photos of her friends, memorabilia from high school dances and concerts, and words and pictures clipped from magazines.

April's side was a completely different story. It looked like the Museum of April. A neat white desk labeled APRIL'S DESK held a stacked plastic file holder that was labeled APRIL'S FILES. The top drawer of the desk was labeled APRIL'S NOTEBOOK PAPER AND SCHOOL SUPPLIES. She even had a small pink book with a lock on it labeled, APRIL'S DIARY— KEEP OUT!

Jade knocked on the doorsill and pointed to a pink plastic cup on her sister's desk. It was labeled APRIL'S PENS AND PENCILS. "Can I borrow a ballpoint pen?"

April paused in her writing. "What for?"

"I'm going to sell it so I can buy a car and run away," Jade answered sarcastically. "What do you think? I'm writing something."

April narrowed her eyes at Jade as she tried to make a decision. Not for the first time, Jade thought how much April looked like a cartoon version of a librarian. Her overlarge eyeglasses magnified her eyes unnaturally. She wore her hair pulled into a tight ponytail at her neck. At last April plucked a blue pen from the cup and held it out to her sister. "I'll need it back when you're finished," she said in a flat voice. "And don't waste the ink."

Jade took the pen with a terse, "Thank you," and once again wondered how it was possible that she and April could ever be sisters. She was certain they didn't have a single chromosome in common.

She hurried back to her hideaway in the garage. With its India-print cloth hanging on the walls and stumps of candles resting on crates and shelves, it looked more like a funky art shop than a place to keep cars. In fact, almost a year had gone by since her mom started parking her car on the street so Jade could have a place to be alone and practice her music.

Jade flopped back down on the lumpy red corduroy couch she'd picked up at Recycled Furniture. She spread a clean sheet of notebook paper on the coffee table, which was really just an old closet door set on cinder blocks, and began to write her letter.

Jade decided to keep it light and breezy. Then she could pretend it was all a joke if Zephyr took it the wrong way.

To Whom It May Concern,
1. This is to inform you that ever since our freshman year, when we brushed shoulders in the hall, I have been:
    a. crazy for you
    b. crazy about shoulders
    c. crazy in general
    d. all of the above
2. For three years I have done nothing about my crush because I am:
    a. a total coward
    b. a hopeless romantic
    c. a complete idiot
    d. all of the above
3. Now that we're seniors, I'd like to change things and:
    a. go out on a limb
    b. go out on a date
    c. go to a music club
    d. do all of the above
4. If you feel the same about me, would you:
    a. write me!
    b. write me!
    c. did I mention, write me?
    d. all of the above
5. If you think this is the dumbest letter you ever read, would you:
    shoot me now.
Jade Chandler

When she was finished, Jade folded the note and tucked it into her pack. Tomorrow, she would give it to Lucy, and her vow to "shoot the moon" would begin.

3

"Any news?" Keesha asked. It was Friday, and the three friends were pushing their trays through the lunch line in the school cafeteria. "Has Lover Boy written back?"

Jade quickly looked over her shoulder to see if any of the two hundred students filling the cafeteria had overheard. "No! And will you stop with the Lover Boy routine?"

"Look who's being sensitive!" Keesha grabbed a plate of cheese nachos and set it on her tray, along with a can of Coke. "There's not a soul in this building who knows who Lover Boy is."

"Except one," Jade corrected her as she took a carton of milk and an apple. "If

You-Know-Who got the letter, then he would know that he's Lover Boy."

"Of course Zephyr got the letter," Lucy blurted as she placed a carton of plain yogurt and a bowl of granola on her tray. "I delivered it to his locker just before school got out yesterday."

The girls paid for their lunches and carried their trays to a table by the window. The cafeteria, with its big windows looking out over the playing fields, was the newest part of the school—and it was twenty years old.

Keesha crunched down on a tortilla chip. "So, how did you know which locker was Zephyr's?" she asked, chewing loudly.

"Duh!" Lucy said as she stirred granola into her yogurt. "His locker number is six-six-six. Everyone knows that."

"That was *last* year," Keesha reminded her. "What about *this* year?"

Lucy paused with her spoon in the air as a look of concern crept across her face. "He has the same locker, doesn't he? I mean, we kept *our* old lockers."

Keesha took a sip of Coke. "We kept ours 'cause we wanted to stay together. Maybe he wanted to change."

Lucy waved her spoon. "Why would he want to change? He had that scary devil's number, which everyone thought was *so* cool."

Keesha shrugged. "I hope you're right."

As Jade listened to their exchange, her stomach did flip-flops. "Did you or did you not deliver that note to Zephyr?" she cut in abruptly.

Lucy jumped and instantly dripped yogurt onto her vintage purple and white polka-dot dress. She grabbed a napkin from the dispenser on the table and dabbed at the stain on her lap. "Zephyr got it, all right? I saw him just before lunch today and he even asked about you."

"Really?" Jade asked, pleased. "What did he say?"

Lucy closed her eyes, trying to remember the exact words. "He said, 'Are you and Jade having lunch on campus or off?'"

"And what did you say?" Jade asked.

Lucy pulled out another paper napkin. "I said, we're staying on campus."

Keesha slammed her Coke can down on the table in surprise. "That's it? I don't believe it."

Jade looked at Keesha. "What's not to believe?"

"He didn't say one word about me!" Keesha put one hand on the waist of her form-fitting suede miniskirt and wobbled her head back and forth. "What am I? Invisible?"

"I can't believe you're thinking about yourself!" Jade said, tossing one of Keesha's nachos at her.

Keesha ducked the flying chip dripping with melted cheese and demanded, "What's your problem? Lover Boy asked about you."

"That's what worries me," Jade said darkly. "What if Zephyr got the letter and asked Lucy if I was going to be in the cafeteria because he *didn't* want to run into me?"

The three girls instinctively swiveled in their seats to look for Zephyr. As they scanned the room, Jade asked, "See him?"

Lucy shook her head. "I'm afraid I don't."

To get a better view, Keesha stood on her chair, wobbling a bit in her high-heeled leather boots. Then she dropped down in her seat when one of the cafeteria workers gave her a "don't do that" gesture. "I hate to say it, Jade, but your boy is out to lunch."

Jade slumped back in her chair, covering her face with her hands. "I knew it. Now he's going to avoid me in the halls and in class." She lowered her hands. "How many more days until school lets out?"

Lucy surprised her with a quick answer. "It's thirteen days until the Battle of the Bands dance, which falls on an early release day. Does that count?"

Keesha's jaw dropped open. "Girl! How'd you know that?"

Lucy blushed. "Chris Sutton and I were talking about it last night. He wants me to go with him."

Lucy's mention of the Battle of the Bands sent a new flurry of butterflies whizzing around Jade's stomach. She didn't know what to worry about more: trying to win a spot in the Battle of the Bands, or Zephyr's response to her letter. "Arrggh," she moaned. "This year is getting more complicated by the second."

The buzzer rang to warn them that lunch period was over and they had ten minutes to get to class. The girls dumped their food in the trash and placed their trays on the big stack by the dishwasher. Then

Keesha led the way to their lockers.

Lucy chattered on about Chris the entire way. "It's amazing we've never met before. We shop at the same co-op. His parents are into drumming. We even went to the Ohio Renaissance Festival in Harveysburg at the same time."

"He sounds as hippie-dippie as you. The perfect match," Keesha said. She stepped back to avoid being bowled over by a trio of girls passing by. "So, when are we going to meet Mr. Granola Guy?"

Lucy slapped Keesha's shoulder playfully. "Never, if you're going to call him that."

"Okay." Keesha shrugged. "So when do we meet the Veg Head?"

"Keesha, stop it!" Lucy squealed.

Normally Jade would have joined in their banter, but she was too nervous about Zephyr. If he had really tried to avoid her at lunch and was now in the hall, she didn't want to bump into him by accident. She peeked out from behind Keesha and spotted Rod Cruz and his skater friends. They were clustered around the pay phone. Sometimes Zephyr hung out with them, but not today.

Zan Teal and Morgan Fifer burst into the

hall through the gym doors. They were rabid Side Effects fans and seldom far from Zephyr or his band. Still no sign of Zephyr. Zan and Morgan waved at Jade as they hurried by. She forced a smile and waved back.

"Jade!" Lucy tugged the back of Jade's pleated tie-dyed miniskirt. "Make Keesha stop. Now she's calling Chris Bok Choy Boy."

Jade walked sideways so she could keep an eye on the gym doors. "Want to shut her up?" she called over her shoulder to Lucy. "Ask her about Kip."

"Now don't start on Kip," Keesha said in a low voice. "I'm over him. Okay?"

"Tell me another," Jade cracked.

Keesha glanced around nervously to see if Kip was nearby, then whispered, "I don't want someone to tell him that I'm calling his name out in the halls. He's already got a big head."

"Okay, then, I won't mention *your* friend"—Lucy paused to take a drink at the water fountain—"if you don't call *mine* names."

"Deal," Keesha said, giving Lucy a high five.

Jade shook her head. "Would you look at us? Wednesday we agreed to let boys into our lives and three days later all we do is fight about them."

"We're not fighting," Keesha protested. "We're discussing." Suddenly Keesha stopped short a few feet from their lockers. "I think I'm having a vision."

Lucy and Jade slammed right into Keesha's back.

"What is it?" Jade felt her nose to see if she'd broken it when she bumped into Keesha.

"There!" Keesha pointed at a slip of folded notebook paper sticking out of the door to Jade's locker. "Is that what I think it is?"

Lucy peeked around Keesha. "That definitely looks like a note." She grinned triumphantly at Jade. "See? I told you Zephyr got the letter!"

Jade could only stare.

"You've got less than five minutes to open that letter and read it." Keesha gave Jade a shove. "Now get a move on, before I do it for you."

Jade snapped out of her daze and hurried over to the old metal locker. The note was definitely for her. Her name was neatly printed on the outside.

"Eeeeee!" Jade squealed, for the second time in two days. She quickly stopped as two girls from her American Poetry class turned to see if something was seriously the matter with her.

"Open it!" Lucy urged as she tried to yank the note out of Jade's hands. "Hurry! The bell's going to ring."

Jade's hands shook as she unfolded the note. Then, in hushed voices, the three of them read the note aloud:

Dear Jade,
You are:
    a. totally amazing
    b. breathtakingly beautiful
    c. incredibly odd . . . for such an amazing and beautiful girl
I am:
    a. ready
    b. willing
    c. waiting for you this afternoon at Harpo's after school
                            Adam Lockhart

"Adam Lockhart!" Keesha and Lucy screamed in unison. "Who's he?"

Jade knew exactly who Adam was. She'd run into him the day before just outside the entrance to the high school. He'd smiled and said hello. "You know Adam," she said. "The guy who wears the derby."

"The cute dork?" Keesha said. "I didn't know his last name was Lockhart."

"I didn't know that was his locker," Lucy moaned.

Jade glanced around to see if Adam was hiding somewhere nearby to watch her read his note. Then she leaned her head against her locker. "This is a disaster!"

Lucy backed away nervously down the hall. "I'm so sorry, Jade," Lucy said, wincing at every word. "I know it's all my fault, but we're going to be late for class." She pointed at the clock on the wall. "Can we talk about this later?"

Before Jade could respond, Lucy turned quickly and disappeared around the corner.

"Chicken!" Keesha yelled after her.

Jade kept her head pressed against the locker, shaking it back and forth. "What am I going to do? What am I going to do?"

Keesha tapped her on the back. "Quit moaning and groaning. I have a plan."

"Tell me quick," Jade said as she reread Adam's note. It was an awfully cute reply to her letter. But she felt terrible about it.

"Stand him up," Keesha said. "Don't go to Harpo's. He'll get the message loud and clear."

"I can't do that," Jade said. "Adam thinks I really like him. It's not his fault the note was delivered to him by mistake." She hung her head, moaning. "I knew I should have written Zephyr's name on the note. I knew it, I knew it!"

Keesha opened her locker, dropped two books into her black vinyl bag, and looped it over her shoulder. "Then write him another note and tell him it was a mistake."

Jade snatched her Comp Lit textbook out of her locker and raced to join Keesha. "Then *he'll* feel like an idiot. I'll have to avoid him for the rest of the year and everything will be icky."

"Look, I'm sorry," Keesha said briskly. "But if you don't want to take my advice, then you have got to go to Harpo's and tell that boy to his face that it was all a big mistake."

A wave of dread spread through Jade's body. "That sounds too awful."

"Here's my class," Keesha said as she

opened the door to Mr. Wing's Computer class. "We'll have to talk later."

"I wish you had never dared me to write that letter," Jade hissed angrily.

"Excuse me?" Keesha shut the door again. "Whose idea was it to play your little game of Truth or Dare? Not mine. Not Lucy's."

"Ms. Kelly? Are you in or out?" Mr. Wing called from inside the classroom. "Make up your mind."

Keesha stuck her head in the door and called, "I'm in, Mr. Wing." Then she whispered to Jade over her shoulder, "I can't believe it. Kip saved me a seat."

Keesha went into the class and closed the door just as the bell rang. The hall was empty, and now Jade was tardy.

She walked to her Comparative Literature class like a condemned prisoner climbing the gallows to her doom. In two hours she would have to muster her courage and go to Harpo's café. She would have to meet Adam and tell him about the dare and the letter, and explain that it was all just a big stupid mistake. There was no other way.

4

Harpo's was the hangout for the "prep-pies" at Wheaton High. Only two blocks from the school, it served up burgers, fries, and Cincinnati's famous chili. The front half looked like the lobby of an old movie theater. Framed posters of classic screwball comedies by the Marx Brothers, Laurel and Hardy, and Charlie Chaplin hung from the walls. The chairs at the booths had been salvaged from an old movie house and were covered in worn red velvet upholstery. One corner held a vintage pop-corn machine, which was always popping, while in the other a projector ran an endless loop of silent movie shorts and newsreels.

The back room at Harpo's was where the

real action took place. Half a dozen pool tables took up the middle of the room. At one end were foosball and air hockey games, bordered by a row of video games and pinball machines. The corners held dimly lit booths filled with couples breaking up or making up.

Jade stood on the sidewalk outside the café and stared through the plate-glass windows at the students inside sipping Cokes and eating fries. She usually made it a point to avoid going into Harpo's. It just felt too gossipy and crowded. But Adam was nowhere to be seen. She shuddered at the thought of having to go into the back room to find him.

"Daunting, isn't it?" a voice murmured in her ear.

Jade nearly jumped out of her skin. Adam was standing beside her, in his trademark derby and tie. "What are you doing there?" she gasped.

"Looking for you," Adam replied, with a lopsided grin. "I'm just relieved that I don't have to run the gauntlet in the game room to find you."

Jade blinked in surprise. "That's funny. I was just thinking the same thing."

Adam tucked a hand in his pocket and leaned against the parking sign. "The truth is, I don't really like Harpo's at all, but it's the only place I could think of to meet."

"Does this mean we don't have to go in?" Jade asked.

Adam looked at her intently. "You don't *have* to do anything."

The thought flashed across Jade's mind that this was the perfect moment to tell Adam the truth about the note and the mix-up.

But the moment came and went.

"It seems that we're in agreement about Harpo's not being the ideal meeting place," Adam continued. "So may I suggest another one?"

Maybe it was the oddly formal way that Adam spoke that intrigued her. Or maybe it was the possibility of discovering a new and interesting café or restaurant. Whatever it was, something made Jade say yes when she knew she probably should have said no.

"But I really can't stay for very long," she added, giving herself an out. "I have a, um, music thing I have to do."

"Fair enough." Adam started down the

sidewalk leading away from Harpo's and the nearby shops. "Let's go."

As Jade walked in silence next to Adam, a voice inside her head screamed, "Tell him! Tell him *now,* before it's too late!" But she couldn't find the words to begin.

After they'd walked a block and a half, Adam paused beside an alley between two brick buildings. "Let's take a short cut," he said. "If you don't mind."

"I don't mind," Jade said politely. Of course, the little voice inside her shouted, "You do *too* mind! Tell him it was all a mistake and get it over with right now."

Jade followed Adam into the narrow passageway. It was a tight squeeze getting around a large green Dumpster and several dented trash cans that partially blocked the entrance.

"I must have walked by here a hundred times," Jade confessed, "but I've never even thought of walking through here." She hopped over a puddle of water and ducked under a clothesline that drooped across the alley.

"I make it a point to walk through alleys," Adam said. "You get to know a building's secrets. For instance"—he pointed up at a rusted metal fire escape crammed with pots full of flowers—"Mrs. Sara Jensen lives there. She's eighty-five. She grows those flowers on her veranda, as she calls it, and then takes them over to patients at the Erie Medical Center."

Jade squinted up at the narrow stretch of blue sky visible between the two buildings. "You'd think those flowers wouldn't get enough sun," she remarked.

"Only Sara's flowers are able to thrive," Adam said. "She must have quite a green thumb."

Jade looked sideways at Adam. He was so . . . thoughtful.

Adam fixed her with a steady gaze. "Of course, there are those who would tell you it's the zoo-doo fertilizer she gets from the Cincinnati Zoo that makes the difference," he said matter-of-factly. "But I prefer to think she has a special way with plants."

She noticed the barest hint of a twinkle appear in his warm brown eyes. He was such a nice guy!

"So, what else can you tell me about this alley?" She twirled around as if she were scoping out a brand-new home.

"Well, a little girl must live close by."
Adam pointed to a pink tricycle tipped over
at the base of the fire escape. "Either that, or
a hobbit," he added. He bent down and
picked up a brass curtain ring from off the
ground.

Jade burst out laughing. "You're a little
weird, Adam."

Adam frowned. "Weird in a good way, or
weird in a weird way?"

She folded her arms across her chest and
studied him. Adam was definitely cute, no
doubt about that. But he was different. It
wasn't just his style of dress that set him
apart. It was more the way he saw the world.

"Maybe a little of both," Jade said at last.

"That's all I can really hope for, consider-
ing we don't really know each other," he
said, touching his hat.

They continued down the alley, and Jade
said, "Can I ask you a question?"

"Only if I get to ask you one," he replied,
as if they were beginning a new game.

"What's with the hat?" She nodded to
his derby. "Why do you wear it?"

"Some might say it keeps my thoughts
from flying away," he said, lifting the black

hat and slamming it back down on his head. "But the real truth is—I just like it."

"Where did you get it?" Jade asked.

"That's more than one question," Adam pointed out, "but I'll answer it, anyway. My parents divorced when I was five, and my mother and I moved from our big house in Cleveland to a miniscule apartment here on the outskirts of Cincinnati. The apartment came furnished with a bed, a couch, a table, two chairs, and one derby."

"The hat was just left in the apartment?" Jade asked.

Adam nodded. "My mother's room had the bed, but my room had the derby. I knew then that I was the lucky one. She may have gotten the bed, but I got the hat. I put it on and slept on the couch."

Jade liked the idea of a little kid in pj's sleeping on a couch in an oversized derby hat. "That's awfully sweet," she said, looking at Adam's hat with new eyes. "Most people have to leave their security blankets at home, but you get to wear yours."

"Exactly." Adam took her hand to help her over a stack of scrap lumber blocking the end of the alley. "I knew you'd see it that way."

They left the narrow passage and stepped onto a sidewalk across from a tiny park. The park was a tidy square of neatly trimmed grass, a single lamppost, and a wrought-iron bench. Jade gasped. "I didn't even know this was here! It's adorable."

Adam jogged across the street and hopped up onto the bench. "Now isn't this better than Harpo's?"

"Way better," Jade said, skipping across to join him. "But I thought we were going to a restaurant."

"I never actually used the restaurant word," Adam corrected. "I suggested we go to a *different* place. However, if you're hungry and wish to eat, maybe we can knock on one of those doors and ask for a sandwich."

Adam waved to the rows of identical buildings that bordered the tiny square. Then he hopped off the bench and started to cross the road.

"No, don't!" Jade cried, grabbing his arm.

Adam spun back around and caught hold of her waist, to keep from knocking into her. For a moment they stood close together, their faces only inches apart. He smelled good. Not heavy with cologne, but fresh and clean.

"Soap," Jade murmured.

"Did you say soap?" Adam asked, keeping his hands on her waist.

Jade's eyes widened in horror. She hadn't realized she'd spoken out loud. "I was thinking that you smelled like soap," she said, backing away in embarrassment.

"So you were . . . sniffing me." His eyes twinkled with amusement.

"Yes. I-I mean, no! Or not on purpose," Jade stammered. This was all too strange. One second she was preparing to tell Adam good-bye forever, and the next she was standing three inches from his face and getting weak-kneed over him. She paced around the little square of grass, wishing there was someplace she could run and hide.

"Gardenias," Adam said, stepping in front of her and stopping her nervous pacing.

"Excuse me?" Jade said.

"You smell like gardenias," Adam said matter-of-factly. "So, now that we have that cleared up, do you want to sit down for a little bit?" He gestured to a grassy spot near the center of the tiny park.

Jade pulled her watch out of her pocket to check the time. The watchband had broken a year before, but she liked the watch face, so she kept it in the pocket of her jeans. "I should really think about going."

"Ah, but you can't go yet," Adam said. "I haven't asked you *my* question."

"Oh, right." Jade dropped onto her knees on the grass. "Ask me." She held her breath, hoping he wouldn't ask her anything like, "What made you decide to write me a letter?" Or, "When did you first notice me?" Or anything she'd have to answer with a lie.

Adam knelt across from her and stroked his chin with one hand, concentrating. Finally he asked, "If you could choose between a life of luxury in only one place, or a life of adventure with just a backpack and no financial guarantees, which would you choose?"

Adam's question so surprised Jade that she burst out laughing. "I thought you were going to ask me something personal."

Adam shrugged. "It's a question about the way you plan to live your life. How much more personal can you get?"

Jade plucked at the grass in front of her. "Well, when you put it that way, I suppose

I'd have to say I'd probably pick the life with the backpack and no money, even though I know how hard it is to live when the money's not there. Mom has her good real estate years and her really terrible we-can-only-afford-macaroni-and-cheese years."

"So, why the backpack and not the security?" Adam asked, removing a black pen and a small spiral notebook from his pocket. He cocked his head like a news reporter, waiting for her answer.

"I read once that Helen Keller said life is either a daring adventure or it is nothing," Jade replied. "I think sitting in one place with lots of money is nothing."

As Jade spoke, Adam began scribbling in his little notebook.

"Are you taking notes?" Jade asked. "Is this some kind of personality quiz?"

"I'm taking notes, but not actually writing any words," Adam replied. He held the book up for her to see. He'd sketched a line drawing of her kneeling in the grass, her head tilted to one side, lost in thought.

"That's awesome," Jade said appreciatively. "You are full of surprises, Adam Lockhart."

"I believe we all are." Adam tore out his drawing and began to fold it. "You, for instance, knocked my socks off with your letter."

Jade took a deep breath. This was definitely *the* moment to tell Adam the truth. But she just couldn't do it. Instead, she hopped to her feet and began slapping blades of grass off the knees of her jeans. "That letter was a real *daring* act for me." Jade put plenty of emphasis on the "dare" part of it. "More of a moment of temporary insanity, really."

Adam stood up and declared seriously, "Those are the moments that make the world go around." He took her hand and placed the drawing, which he had folded into the shape of a bird, onto her palm. "So, can I walk you to wherever it is you need to be?"

Jade studied the small paper bird in her hand. Adam was odd. He spoke and acted unlike any boy she'd ever met. Was that a good thing? She didn't know.

Adam waved his hand slowly across her line of vision. "Hel-lo? Didn't you say you needed to be someplace?"

Jade looked up, startled. "Why, yes, I

think I did. Shall we walk back to Harpo's?"

She started to head back toward the alley, but Adam caught hold of her elbow. "Never backtrack. Always move forward." He grinned and added, "So allow me to show you Bramble Lane." Adam took off his derby and gestured toward a side street angling away from the park. "It's on our way."

"I know Bramble Lane," Jade replied. "My mother sold a house there last May. It's lined with cherry trees that are really beautiful in the spring."

"Those trees are spectacular," Adam agreed as they walked down the sidewalk under a canopy of leafy branches. "Even now in the fall, while they've still got their leaves. But what I want to show you is up here on our right."

They passed two trim Cape Cod–style homes with manicured lawns. Then Adam turned and led Jade up the driveway of a small yellow cottage. The front lawn, which was bordered by a white picket fence, was filled with wildflowers. Adam walked confidently around the side of the house toward the backyard.

"Do you know who lives here?" Jade whispered as she followed.

"No," Adam whispered back. "Who?"

Jade looked nervously toward the front porch, checking to see if anyone was looking out the window. "Won't the owners be upset if they see us?"

"We'll find out," Adam whispered back. "But whatever happens, it will be worth the journey."

The rear of the small cottage opened onto a tiny wooded area filled with rocks, wildflowers, trees, and a small stream. Scattered between the rocks and under the trees were tiny painted gnomes.

Jade clasped her hands together and gasped in delight. "I had no idea this was here! How did you find it?"

"I used to work as a paper boy," Adam explained. "One day I overthrew the Hansons' driveway"—he gestured with his thumb to the big gray and white house on the right—"and the paper went into this house's backyard. When I went to retrieve the newspaper, I found this. Amazing, huh?"

"I wonder what the story is on the gnomes?" Jade chuckled. "Are they supposed to be the Seven Dwarfs or something? And that one statue of the girl sitting on that bench and feeding the bird could be Snow White."

Adam nodded. "It's very possible. I've always thought the one with the glasses is Doc. Usually he's over by the gate, but I see he's decided to stand by the stream today."

Jade gasped. "Someone moves the gnomes around every day?"

Adam held up one finger. "I didn't say that, but their locations do change. You can draw your own conclusions."

They heard a door shut inside the yellow house, and Adam caught hold of Jade's hand. "That sounds like our cue to leave."

Ducking under the picture window of the yellow house, they scurried down the driveway and across the street. They ran with their heads thrown back, laughing. Adam started whistling the "Heigh-Ho!" song, and that only made them laugh harder.

They ran all the way back to Ohio Avenue, and Harpo's. Then the two of them collapsed against the side of the building, giggling.

Jade couldn't remember when she'd had more fun just walking around the block. She was about to tell Adam that, when a familiar voice cut in.

"Jade! There you are," Keesha said. "Lucy and I have been tearing this town apart looking for you!"

The urgent tone in Keesha's voice made Jade stop laughing instantly. "Why? What's the matter? Did I forget something?"

"Yes! Your date! Hello?" Keesha said, giving Jade a meaningful look.

Jade frowned. "Date?"

Keesha rolled her eyes and gestured sideways with her head at Adam. "Remember? You told me to remind you about that *date* you had *tonight*?" Keesha overemphasized "date" and "tonight."

Jade realized Keesha was trying to give Jade an easy excuse to get away from Adam. Instead, she was creating an embarrassing situation.

Adam got what was going on right away. "Well, thanks, Jade," he said quickly. "It's been fun. I'm sure I'll catch you later." He tipped his hat and backed down the street.

"Wait!" Jade started to run after him,

but Keesha pulled on her sleeve.

"Girl!" Keesha hissed. "Don't run after that boy. I'm trying to help you out, remember?"

"You don't have to be so rude!" Jade hissed back. She turned to say good-bye, but Adam was gone. She stepped out onto Ohio Avenue and looked up and down the street.

"How'd he do that?" Jade murmured. "One second he was here, and the next second he was gone." She snapped her fingers. "Like that."

Keesha shrugged. "Isn't that what you wanted?"

Jade didn't answer. This crazy afternoon with Adam had turned her world upside down. At this moment, she wasn't sure what she wanted.

"I don't like lying to people," Jade muttered. "I don't have a date tonight."

"But you do have one tomorrow," Keesha reminded her. "With me at the Atomic Café. So that's not really lying. It's stretching the truth a little bit."

"It's just that . . . well, Adam's a nice guy." Jade chewed the tip of one fingernail and continued to stare in the direction where he'd disappeared. "I hope he's not mad."

Keesha frowned. "You *did* tell him about the mix-up, didn't you?"

"Not exactly." Jade winced and waited for Keesha to scream at her—which she did.

"What! You let him think that note was written to *him*?" Keesha clapped one hand to her head and marched up and down the sidewalk in front of Harpo's. "That beats everything. Wait until Lucy hears this one."

Jade took her friend by the shoulders. "Don't make a big deal of this, Keesha. I just never found the right moment to tell him. But I'm going to call him this weekend."

"You'd better," Keesha said, shaking her finger at Jade. "Because the longer you wait, the bigger the break is going to be in that boy's heart."

Suddenly Jade and Keesha got the distinct feeling they were being watched. They slowly turned their heads to look over at Harpo's. Courtney Kass and Caitlin Winters were standing at the window, along with several other horribly catty girls at Wheaton High. They looked like they were getting a big charge out of watching Jade and Keesha argue.

Jade stuck her tongue out at them. Keesha did the same, which made the two girls explode into giggles.

"I think I'll be running along now," Jade said, wiping tears of laughter from her eyes. "This has been an amazingly full day, and I've got a lot to do tonight."

"Remember, eight o'clock tomorrow, Atomic Café," Keesha said. She extended her pinkie and thumb and pretended to hold a phone to her ear. "And don't forget to call You-Know-Who!"

5

On Saturday, Keesha went over early to see if Jade had made her call to Adam. She hadn't. They spent the afternoon arguing about the situation and then everything else. Even Jade's mom noticed it.

"You girls need a break from each other," she commented after listening to them wrestle over the milk carton. "You are both way too cranky."

Keesha let go of the carton and followed Mrs. Chandler down the hall. "Talk to your daughter," she complained. "That girl has been a royal pain all afternoon."

Jade knew that she hadn't been the perfect host, but she was angry with Keesha for being so pushy. Finally Jade told Keesha that yes, she would call Adam. When *she* was ready.

After that, Keesha let up on the "Adam" issue and turned her focus to the evening ahead. The two friends actually had fun getting dressed. Even though it was just a regular music night at the Atomic Café, they decided to really go wild.

Jade, who practically lived in her shredded jeans, traded them in that evening for a pair of red fishnet stockings and a sheer, black baby doll dress. She set a tiny sparkly tiara on top of her straight magenta hair.

Keesha suggested Jade wear heels, but she said, "No. Too girly." Instead, Jade slipped her feet into her favorite green Doc Martens with the rainbow laces. "Just right."

Keesha had brought a suitcase full of choices with her. After trying on several outfits she finally announced, "Tonight I am going super-styley."

"Styley" in Keesha's world meant straight mini, high heels, and form-hugging cashmere sweater. The sweater and skirt were a burnt orange, which looked fabulous next to her caramel-colored skin.

Getting dressed took them nearly two hours, which is why they were almost fifteen minutes late when they arrived at the Atomic Café.

The Atomic Café was located near a freeway overpass in a long, low building that was once a bowling alley. The building was painted black and dappled with planets and stars in bright neon yellows, pinks, and purples. No one knew who had painted it. The mural just appeared one day, just like the others that had popped up on other buildings around Wheaton. As a joke, the newspapers had named the mysterious vandals who'd painted it Art Attack.

Even though it was only eight fifteen, the parking lot was jammed with cars when Jade turned her brother's red Jeep Wrangler into it. Nick had loaned his convertible to her just for the evening. It was fifteen years old and covered in rust and dents, but Jade loved it.

"Ooh. There's an open space," Keesha said, pointing to a vacant spot by the overpass.

Lucy was standing where she said she'd

be, right by the electric marquee announcing that week's lineup of bands. A tall, thin boy with shaggy blond hair stood beside her.

"That has got to be Chris Sutton, the Granola Guy," Keesha murmured as they parked the Jeep and hurried toward the club. "He's got his hippie boy outfit down."

Chris was wearing a bleached-linen shirt, a loose paisley vest, drawstring pants, and Birkenstock sandals. Lucy was in a patchwork jumper with a bleached-linen blouse underneath, and matching Birkenstocks.

"They look like twins," Keesha commented.

Jade agreed with Keesha but nudged her with her elbow. "Go easy on the guy," she whispered. "Lucy really likes him."

"Well, no wonder," Keesha replied. "They look like Woodstock Barbie and Ken."

Jade snorted with laughter, but stopped herself. "Really, Keesha. Don't be mean!"

"What's with the 'don't be mean' stuff?" Keesha said out of the corner of her mouth. "You act like I'm some kind of grizzly bear."

"Shark is more like it," Jade replied. "Poor Adam didn't have a chance with you."

"Adam!" Keesha gasped, stopping in the

middle of the drive. "I hardly said one word to that boy."

Jade tapped the tip of her nose with her finger. "Exactly. You cut him dead."

"How do you like that?" Keesha raised her arms to the sky in protest. "I try to do my girlfriend a favor and she calls me names."

Lucy had watched their entire exchange from the front steps of the Atomic Café. "Are you two coming into the club," she called, "or are you just going to stand out there and fight?"

"Who's fighting?" Keesha said, sashaying in her black patent-leather heels toward Lucy and Chris. "We're just having a difference of opinion. I happen to be right. And Jade happens to be wrong."

Jade jogged easily past Keesha up beside Chris and whispered in an exaggerated voice, "Don't listen to her. She's really losing it." She twirled her finger in a circle by her head. "Early onset dementia."

"Excuse me?" Keesha stepped in front of Jade. "But it's Miss Jade who wins the Loony Toon award."

Chris, who seemed like a really easygoing guy, chuckled at their antics. Lucy beamed with happiness as she looped her arm through his and said, "Chris, I'd like you to meet my very best friends, Jade and Keesha."

Chris shook hands and drawled in a soft Southern accent, "Pleased to meet you. Lucy warned me about you both, and I see she was right." He winked at Lucy. "They *are* insane."

Jade liked him instantly. He really did seem like the perfect boy for Lucy. She glanced sideways at Keesha, who gave him an approving nod.

Lucy and Chris led the girls inside the Atomic Café. First they had to stop at the front podium to pay the five-dollar cover charge. As Jade waited for JoJo, the heavyset bouncer and part owner of the club, to stamp her hand, she looked around the place. Most of the tables were already filled with teens from Wheaton, Deerfield, and Mt. Airy.

Six guys were at a table near the dance floor, talking and laughing loudly over the recorded music. Lucy spotted them first and sang out, "Oh, Kee-sha! You'll never guess who's he-ere!"

Keesha peeked her head out from behind Lucy. "Kip?"

Lucy pointed to two beefy guys from the Wheaton High football team. "He's over there, with R.J. and Sam Lennox."

Keesha pulled her fist into her side and kicked up one heel. "Yes!"

She bounced in time with the music as she wove her way through the crowd toward Kip's table. Jade followed, whispering, "I thought you were done with Kip because he dropped you."

"I didn't exactly say I was *done*," Keesha demurred. "He saved me a seat all week in CAD class, but I ignored him. So now he's interested in me again."

Jade frowned. "That sounds like major game-playing to me."

"That's right. It's the game of love," Keesha said with a toss of her head. "And right now I'm winning."

Keesha pushed ahead and joined Kip at his table in a flurry of greetings. Jade hung back. She didn't feel like getting anywhere near the competitors in "the game of love." Looking around, she saw that Lucy and Chris had already found a table in a darkened corner. They were huddled together with their foreheads touching, deep in conversation.

Suddenly Jade felt like two's company and three's a crowd with both Lucy and Keesha. Rather than sit down with either friend, she decided to go to the snack bar and wait for the live music to begin.

Promptly at eight thirty, a spotlight lit the center mike on the bandstand. When JoJo stepped up to the microphone, a rowdy cheer went up from the crowd.

"Looks like we've got an awesome lineup tonight," he announced into the microphone. "And a totally hot crowd!"

Another cheer sounded from the audience, especially the table with Keesha, Kip, and the Lennox brothers. As JoJo listed the groups who were to play that evening, a leather-clad figure slipped into the spot next to Jade at the drink counter.

"Glad to see you could make it," Zephyr rumbled in his husky voice.

Jade nearly jumped out of her skin. "Zephyr!" she gasped. "I didn't know you were here. I mean, I-I knew you were *here*," she continued to stammer, "but not *here* at the counter."

A smile crept slowly across Zephyr's lips. He seemed pleased to see her so flustered. "I thought I'd play 'In Your Eyes,' the song we jammed on in Mr. C's class. What do you think?"

Zephyr fixed her with his piercing blue eyes. He'd never really looked at her so intently before, and that made Jade even more nervous. "I think that would be very cool," she said, tucking a strand of hair behind one ear. "I like the harmony we put on the bridge of the song. Can Charlie sing that with you?"

"We'll see," Zephyr said as he ordered a can of Red Bull and a bottle of water. "If not, maybe you can sit in with us."

"Me?" Adrenaline shot through Jade's body as she thought of performing onstage with Zephyr and Side Effects. She'd dreamed about this moment! "I'd love it!" she finally choked out.

Zephyr touched her elbow with his hand. "Cool. I'll see you on the ice."

Jade leaned casually against the counter and watched him carry his drinks into the backstage area. As soon as he was out of sight, she hopped up and down with excitement. She couldn't wait to tell her friends. Jade finished the rest of her soda in one swig and hurried back to the dance floor to find Lucy and Chris.

She raced to the set of tables by the wall, but they were no longer there. Jade spun back around and hurried toward Keesha's table by the stage, just as the Phreeze, a hot new band from Cincinnati, started playing.

Keesha and Kip grabbed hands and raced onto the dance floor. Jade watched them nod and sway to the music. Keesha was a great dancer, and Kip was very aware of it. This was not the moment to bust in between them and share her good news.

Jade flopped down in the nearest empty chair. Who could she tell about the impromptu gig?

Adam's face instantly popped into her mind. She remembered the way his brown eyes looked at her when she spoke. They were warm, understanding, and open. Maybe she should call him!

Jade hopped to her feet. Why not? She owed him an apology, and this would be a good time to deliver it. Good and bad news together. Jade pulled her cell phone out of her pack and went out to the parking lot to make the call.

First she had to call information. Of course she didn't know Adam's mother's name, but she figured there couldn't be that many Lockharts in Wheaton. The operator gave her the number, and she dialed.

A boy's voice answered. "You rang?"

"Adam? It's me, Jade," she said, trying to talk over the noise of the music spilling out into the parking lot.

"Yes, I know," he replied. "I have Caller ID. Who else would be calling me from their cell?"

Suddenly she felt awkward and couldn't really remember why she had thought it was a good idea to call him. She was supposed to be letting him down.

"I know you're there," he said finally. "I can hear you breathing."

That made Jade laugh, and she said, "I wanted to apologize for yesterday afternoon."

"Why?" Adam asked. "I had a great time."

"Oh, I did too," Jade assured him. "It's just that when we got back to Harpo's and ran into Keesha, things got weird and I didn't get to say good-bye."

"So that's why you called?" Adam asked. "To say good-bye?"

Jade shook her head, giggling. "Adam, you are too funny. Actually the reason I called was I just found out I'm going to be singing with Side Effects tonight at the Atomic Café, and I wanted to share the good news."

"Congratulations!" Adam sounded genuinely happy for her. "Would you like me to come cheer for you?"

"No!" Jade shouted, a little too loudly.

"All right, I won't," Adam said immediately.

Jade knew Adam shouldn't come to the club. Her friends wouldn't really understand, and Keesha might be rude again. It might even ruin her future with Zephyr. But how could she tell Adam that? She quickly tried to backpedal. "I think I'd be too nervous with you in the audience," she said, exaggerating the truth.

"My mother used to feel the same way," Adam cracked. "But I stopped running up and down the aisles when I was six. I promise I'll stay in my seat the whole time."

For a fraction of a second Jade thought it might be fun to have Adam there. But she still wasn't sure about her feelings for

Zephyr. "No," she said firmly. "I'd rather you didn't this time."

"I guess I'll just have to hold out for a private concert," Adam said with a sigh. "What do you say to a picnic tomorrow? I'll bring the lunch, you bring the music."

"That sounds like fun," Jade replied, without hesitating.

"I'll pick you up," Adam said. "And if it's all right with you, I've got a few people I'd like you to meet."

"Hey, I thought this was going to be a private concert," Jade joked.

"Don't worry," Adam said. "I trust them with my life. You can trust them with your music."

It all sounded very mysterious and interesting. Jade would have liked to ask more questions, but just then JoJo's voice came blasting over the loudspeakers. "Thank you, ladies and germs, that was the Phreeze. Now, don't get too comfortable. Our next band really rocks. Let's give it up for Wheaton High's one and only . . . Side Effects!"

The applause from the crowd inside the club was so loud that Jade couldn't hear

Adam. She plugged her open ear with a finger and shouted into the phone, "Listen, Adam, I'm really sorry, but I have to go. Side Effects just hit the stage."

"Break a leg!" Adam shouted into the phone.

Jade couldn't hear him. "What?"

"Good luck!" Adam said. "Just be glad I'm not there in the audience. I have a feeling I *would* have been running up and down the aisles cheering."

Jade quickly gave him her phone number and address for the picnic, and then raced back into the Atomic Café.

Zephyr was at the microphone, playing the intro to the band's signature tune, "Big Trouble Ahead." He saw her as she found a place near the center back and nodded. She waved a quick hello. Then Zephyr launched into the opening lyrics:

"Caught by surprise one summer day,
The lady in red, she looked my way.
The blood started rushing to my head,
I should have turned away from the lady
    in red."

As the drummer, Mac Holloway, kicked into a driving back beat, Lucy suddenly appeared beside Jade. "I saw Zephyr give you that look," she said, cupping her hand to talk in Jade's ear.

"What look?" Jade asked innocently.

"You know what look," Lucy said, trying to shout over the music. "The one that said, 'You're the one I was waiting for. This song is for you.'"

Jade laughed. "Lucy, Zephyr saw me come in and he nodded in my direction. That's all."

"Uh-huh," Lucy said knowingly.

Then Zephyr stepped back to the mike and sang the chorus to "Big Trouble Ahead."

"Whoa, big boy, big trouble ahead,
Better back off, she'll go to your head.
She'll mess with your heart, and
    you'll wish you were dead,
Stay away, stay away from the lady
    in red."

He grabbed the microphone and, leaning forward, directed the entire song to

Jade. Lucy, of course, saw this and, squealing with excitement, jabbed Jade in the ribs with her elbow over and over again.

"Cut it out," Jade hissed out of the side of her mouth. All around her, people turned in their chairs to see just who Zephyr was singing to. Jade tried to look composed and cool, but she could feel her cheeks blazing a bright red.

When the song ended, Jade clapped enthusiastically, but Lucy was hopping up and down, cheering. Soon she was joined by Keesha, who poked Jade a few more times with her elbow. "I saw that," she teased. "Girl, Zeph likes you!"

Jade clutched her aching sides. She didn't think she could survive any more "support" from her friends. "Will you two calm down?" she said. "You're making us look like a bunch of groupies."

Keesha's jaw dropped. "Lucy here may have acted a little nuts, but no way am I a groupie. I am always ultra cool." She snapped her fingers.

Jade burst out laughing. "No one in this group is cool, Keesha. Lucy has been giggling all night because of Chris. And I'm sure it was you I saw drooling all over Kip."

Keesha put both hands on her hips, ready to shoot back a reply, when Zephyr's voice interrupted her. "Hey, Jade Chandler."

She looked up at the stage to see him pointing at her. Then he asked, "Why don't you come up here and join us for the next tune?"

When they realized everyone in the place was staring at them, Keesha and Lucy plastered phony smiles on their faces and waved. Jade squeezed their hands and murmured, "Wish me luck."

Keeping her face frozen in a tight smile, Keesha mumbled, "I would. But you don't need it."

Jade ran down the aisle toward the stage. For the briefest moment the thought of a six-year-old Adam in a derby running down the aisles flashed through her mind. It made her laugh, which made her knotted stomach muscles relax.

When she reached the lip of the stage, Zephyr held out his hand and pulled her up to join him.

"You ready?" he murmured as Charlie handed her Zeph's backup guitar.

"I'd better be," she cracked, running her fingers up and down the neck to warm up. She nodded to Zephyr, and he introduced the next song. "Here's an old tune with a new twist. Jade and I hope you like it."

The lights shifted, and the two of them shared the mike in a small circle of blue light. As Zephyr began to play, the fear flowed out of Jade like water down a drain. This was where she belonged. Onstage. Playing music. Then they began to sing together.

Jade had sung with Zephyr in class, but nothing prepared her for the way they sounded together. It was breathtaking, as if two voices had become part of the same instrument. She seemed to know instinctively where he'd pause to breathe, when he'd lift a line—and she built her harmony around his melody perfectly.

They sang through the last verse facing each other, looking into each other's eyes:

"In your eyes, in your eyes,
Oh, I want to be that complete,
I want to touch the light,
The heat I see in your eyes."

At first the crowd was silent. Then the applause began—and it was deafening.

Zephyr's eyes shone as he took Jade by the hand and raised her arm high in the air, like a winner in the ring. She was grinning so hard, she felt like her cheeks would crack from being stretched so hard. As the cheers rang in her ears, Jade looked at Zephyr and mouthed silently, "Thanks."

He threw back his head and laughed. Then they both took another bow. It was the best night of her entire life.

6

"Ready or not, I'm coming in!" a voice called from somewhere near the door of the garage studio.

Jade put a pillow over her head and buried her face in the couch. "Stop yelling. It's the middle of the night."

Her big toe was sticking out from under the faded blue blanket. April gave it a sharp tug and said, "It's nearly noon. You'd better get up."

"Ouch!" Jade kicked her sister's hand away with both feet. "Why?"

"You've got a visitor," April replied.

"What?" Jade tossed the pillow off her head and squinted at the alarm clock on the end table beside the couch. "What day is this?"

Then a male voice answered, "Sunday."

Adam Lockhart was standing beside April at the end of the couch.

"Adam?" Jade bolted upright on the couch. Her tangled hair flopped down over her face. Her eyes felt swollen and puffy. The torn T-shirt she'd pulled from the dirty clothes to use as a nightshirt completely clashed with her boxer shorts.

April and Adam stared down at her solemnly. "I told you it might be bad," April said.

Adam nodded. "I've seen worse."

"Arrrgh!" Jade pulled the blanket over her head and screamed, "April! I'm going to kill you!"

Jade's mom stuck her head into the room. "What's all the bellowing about?"

"Mother!" Jade answered from under the blanket. "April brought Adam in here and I'm not even dressed."

Mrs. Chandler was unsympathetic. "Then get dressed. We'll entertain Adam in the kitchen."

"Thanks, Mrs. Chandler," Jade heard Adam reply. "But I've already been entertained."

"Get out!" Jade screeched. "Everybody. Including you, Adam Lockhart!"

"All right, troops," Mrs. Chandler said. "You heard her. The viewing is over."

Jade stayed under the blanket and listened as they walked out of the garage and back into the house. She heard her mother scold her sister, "April, let's hope Jade never does that to you when you're older. . . ."

"Mother!" April protested. "In the first place, I would remember the time. And in the second place, I would never oversleep. And third, I wouldn't be caught dead on that filthy couch."

The door clicked shut, and Jade slowly lowered the blanket. She was filled with regret for saying yes to a picnic today. So much had happened since that call with Adam.

She flopped back against the couch, reliving the fun she'd had at the Atomic Café the night before. After Jade had sung with Zephyr, the band invited her to join them on their break. Several people stopped by the table to compliment her. Some even suggested she join Zephyr's band. He didn't exactly leap at the suggestion, but he didn't say no, either. When it was time for the band's next set, Zephyr said good-bye and promised to call her.

Jade's friends were as excited about the evening as she'd been. Lucy and Chris, who had already become a couple, in Jade's mind, both hugged her a lot. As for Keesha, she kept announcing to anyone who would listen, "Jade rocks!"

When Jade drove Keesha home, they put the top down on Nick's jeep and sang "Big Trouble Ahead" at the top of their lungs all the way to Keesha's house. Jade was so pumped up, she couldn't get to sleep. She went out to the garage studio and played her guitar. Then she decided to record her audition song for the Battle of the Bands on her cassette deck. She finally finished at two in the morning. At last she pulled a blanket over herself and fell asleep on the couch.

"I don't want to go on a picnic," Jade groaned as she rolled off the couch. "Why do I have to go on a picnic?" She stumbled over to the round mirror hanging on the wall

beside the washing machine, and gasped.
She looked worse than she thought. Her
mascara was smudged in big black smears
under her eyes, and her hair was suffering
from a terminal case of bedhead.

"You should really take a shower," she
told her reflection. But then Adam would
have to wait longer and her hair would be
wet for the picnic. Jade decided to skip the
shower. She would just throw on some
clothes and get the picnic over with.

Jade washed her face quickly in the laun-
dry sink. Then she grabbed a pair of under-
wear from the pile of folded clothes on top of
the dryer and pulled a pair of striped overalls
from the box marked GOODWILL. She slipped
a pink Donnas concert tee over her head.

"A brush!" Jade mumbled, looking
under the couch and in her backpack. "Why
can't I ever find a brush?"

She finally found a comb on the shelf above
the washer. The tangle in her hair proved to be
too much to deal with, so she pulled it into a
ponytail and tied it with a bandanna. Her Doc
Martens completed her look.

"There!" she said, staring at her reflection. "I'm done."

The girl staring back at her looked like a bleary-eyed farm girl. But what did Adam expect, after bursting into her room while she was asleep? Other girls she knew, like Keesha, would never have spoken to him again for the rest of his life.

When Jade came into the kitchen she was shocked to find Adam, her mom, and her brother, Nick, sitting at the kitchen table playing Slapjack. Adam was the dealer, and her mom and Nick were slapping and scooping the cards into piles as fast as Adam could deal them. Each triumph was accompanied with a "Gotcha!" or "Mine!"

Jade leaned against the doorsill and watched in amazement. First of all, she'd never seen her mother or brother play cards before. She was surprised that they even knew the game of Slapjack. And second of all, Adam was a total stranger, yet here they were acting like he was a member of the family.

"Adam!" Jade called. "I'm sorry I—"

"Can't talk," Adam said, cutting her off. "Must concentrate."

Jade's mom slammed her hand down on a jack of hearts and yelled, "Mine! Get some orange juice from the fridge, Jade. I picked some up this morning."

Jade shrugged and did as she was told. She poured herself a drink and leaned against the kitchen counter. She watched as Adam, his derby tilted off his forehead, expertly flipped the cards in rapid-fire succession. When the game was done, Nick held up both fists in triumph. "The winner and all-time Slapjack champion."

"All-time?" Adam repeated, scooping up the cards and putting them back in the box. "I believe *I* am the bearer of that title."

"Prove it," Nick said, ready to go again.

Jade slammed her juice glass down on the table. "No way. I didn't drag myself out of bed just to watch you three play cards. And where did they come from, anyway?"

Adam tipped his hat. "I'm never without them. You never know when the need for a quick game of Gin Rummy or Slapjack might arise."

Jade's mother patted Adam on the shoulder and said to Jade, "I like this boy. He can come to our house anytime."

"Thanks, Kit," Adam said, calling Jade's mom by her first name. He dropped the deck of cards into his pocket. "Next time we'll try something a little harder, like Go Fish."

"It's a date!" Kit replied.

"And speaking of dates," Adam said as he scooted his chair back and stood up, "Jade and I have one with a very special group of people."

Jade winced. "I forgot about meeting your friends. I thought we were just going on a picnic." She pointed to her overalls. "Should I change?"

Adam stared at her face, tilting his head first to the right, then the left. He never once looked at her clothes. Finally he announced, "Absolutely not. I like you just the way you are."

She shook her head, chuckling. "No, I mean my clothes."

"Oh, those." Adam looked at her overalls. "Are they comfortable?"

"They are," Jade replied.

"Then no need to change," Adam said, smiling warmly. He held up one finger. "However, you did promise to bring your guitar."

"Oh, that's right." Jade ran back to the

garage to get her acoustic guitar. It had a gig bag with shoulder straps, which let her carry it like a backpack. She got back to the kitchen just as the phone rang.

"If that's Mike Mullins asking about his eyesore," Kit Chandler shouted to anyone who would listen, "I'm not here."

"Eyesore?" Adam repeated.

Jade heard her brother explain to Adam as the phone continued to ring, "Eyesore is what my mother calls the old warehouse at the end of Erie Avenue. She's trying to sell it, but it's so ugly, no one wants to buy it."

April finally answered the phone. "Jade!" she shouted at the top of her lungs. "Some guy named Zephyr wants to speak to you."

As Jade raced to grab the phone from April, her sister said, "What kind of name is Zephyr, anyway?"

"It's the ancient Greek name for the West Wind," Jade hissed, covering the mouthpiece with her hand. "And most people think it's very cool."

April shrugged. "Not me."

She took the phone into the hall outside the kitchen to get a little privacy. Unfortunately, Adam and Jade's family were still in the kitchen, ready to say good-bye, so they became an audience for Jade's entire conversation. She tried her best to keep it short and noncommittal.

"Jade, I was wondering if you would like to come over and jam with the band," Zephyr said in his gravelly voice.

"I would like that," Jade replied stiffly. It was hard to be overenthusiastic with four people listening to her every word.

"So how about today at four?" Zephyr asked.

"That would be fine," Jade said politely.

"Cool," Zephyr replied. There was a pause. "Do you know where I live?"

"Not exactly," Jade said. "Could you tell me?"

She felt like an idiot. She didn't have a piece of paper, but she didn't want to ask for one. Then her family would know she'd just made a date to meet another boy while Adam was standing three feet from her.

"It's 357 Sycamore Way," Zephyr said. "We're in the studio in the back."

"Got it," Jade said. Then she added, "Well, um, thanks. And I'll see you."

"Sure." Zephyr sounded a little confused by her lack of enthusiasm. "Four o'clock."

"Bye now," Jade said. She clicked off the phone and handed it back to her sister.

"'Bye now'?" April repeated. "Even I don't say that."

April was right. Only mothers said "bye now." She was going to have to do a lot of fast-talking to make up for the lamest phone call on the planet. She glanced up at the clock. It was 12:45. Only three hours until she would be jamming with Side Effects!

She glanced back at Adam, who was watching her face intently. Had he read her thoughts? She hoped not. He seemed to be such a nice guy. His timing was just off.

"Sorry, Adam," Jade said. "It was a job thingie."

"No problem," Adam said as they headed for the front door. "Those thingies can be pretty important." He turned and waved good-bye to her family. "Kit! It was great. Nick, don't get too attached to that championship title. And April—T.T.F.N!"

"T.T.F.N?" April repeated, confused.

"Ta ta for now!" Adam said, smiling.

Once they were outside of the house,

Jade looked around for Adam's Dodge minivan. But there was no car in the driveway. Instead, a bicycle built for two was leaning against the garage door. The tandem bike was old, with faded green paint on the fenders and a white wicker basket on the front handlebars. The basket was filled with picnic supplies.

"I hope you know how to ride a bike," Adam said as he wheeled the bicycle in front of Jade. "Because those pedals aren't just for show."

Jade giggled as she swung onto her bicycle seat and adjusted her guitar bag on her back. Then she grabbed hold of her set of handlebars. "I've always wanted to ride one of these," she said. "Where did you find it?"

"It belongs to a friend of mine named Vivian," Adam said, hopping onto the front seat. "She thought it was the perfect mode of transportation for a picnic."

"Vivian?" Jade repeated. It sounded like an old-fashioned name.

"You'll meet her soon enough," Adam said with a grin. "Ready?"

Jade gulped hard. She was a little freaked out riding around with Adam like this in such a public way. But she really did want to try the bike. "Ready as I'll ever be."

Adam pushed down on his pedal, and they were off. Jade pedaled in tandem with Adam. When they reached the corner of Ash and Elm, they took the turn a bit wide. Jade tried to follow Adam's moves, leaning when he leaned and sitting straight when he was upright. They quickly developed a rhythm.

"I think we've got it!" Adam called.

"This is fun!" Jade threw her head back, enjoying the cool feel of the wind on her face.

"Fun is for amateurs," Adam said, leaning forward over the handlebars and pedaling faster. "We're here for adventure!"

They cut across Jade's neighborhood and were soon traveling along the edge of Swedenburg Park. They passed joggers, mothers pushing baby carriages, and other cyclists. Everyone they passed smiled and waved. Jade called out, "Good afternoon!" or, "Howdy!"

They cycled past the playground and community pool, which was closed for the season. Jade was certain they would stop by the picnic benches, but Adam kept pedaling. He steered them to the far end of the park, where a water-fall cascaded into a small pond filled with wood ducks, mallards, and a pair of swans. Big gray boulders surrounded the waterfall.

"This spot look good to you?" Adam called over his shoulder.

"Perfect," Jade replied. "And I'm perfectly starved."

As soon as she said it, Jade realized she really was hungry. She hadn't eaten a thing since the night before.

Stopping the tandem bike was a little more difficult then starting it. "On the count of three," Adam instructed, "we'll brake and hop down."

But when he got to two, he accidentally braked too hard. The bike lurched out of control, and they hopped off at different times. The bike clattered over on its side, and they tumbled onto the grass. Jade was able to slip her arms out of the guitar bag before she hit the ground. Her guitar flopped harmlessly on the ground, and she rolled down the hill, giggling all the way.

When Jade came to rest, she took a moment to catch her breath. She lay comfortably on her back in the grass, watching big fluffy white clouds sail by overhead. Adam, whose shoulder was touching hers, must have been doing the same thing, because suddenly he announced, "An elephant. That one looks like an elephant."

He pointed at a mass of white cotton balls with a long white trunk. "I see it," Jade cried. Another cloud sailed by, and she declared, "Mr. Phelps, Art teacher. See? That's his frizzy hair and his pointy nose."

"Brilliant!" Adam responded. "I even see the mole on his cheek."

Jade turned her head to look at Adam, and he did the same. Their faces were only inches apart. It was funny, but Jade didn't feel the least bit uncomfortable. She studied his face as she had the clouds, slowly, taking her time. Adam's brown eyes, she noticed, had a dark rim around them. And his nose was really a nice straight nose with a tiny freckle near the tip. His lips, she found herself thinking, were very kissable.

Adam was in the same dreamy state. His gaze followed the arch of her eyebrows, traveled over her cheeks to her mouth, and back to her eyes again.

Jade realized that she'd probably like it a

lot if Adam kissed her at that moment. She held her breath, wondering what would happen next. Finally, Adam spoke. "Vivian," he murmured.

Jade blinked in surprise. "Who's Vivian?"

Adam raised himself up on one elbow and pointed behind her. "That lady circling the pond."

Jade turned and sat up. Coming toward them was a large, white-haired lady in hiking shorts and boots. Following her were four other elderly people. One man carried two camp stools. Another walked with a cane. One lady carried a wicker picnic basket, and the other a parasol.

"What are they doing?" Jade asked.

Adam waved to the group and said, "They're joining us for lunch."

7

"You must be Jade," an ancient lady in a yellow knit pantsuit and flowered scarf called from the little band of old people inching their way along the edge of the pond. "I'm Dolly."

Jade was still in shock about learning her picnic with Adam was to be shared with some refugees from a senior center. She raised her hand stiffly and called, "Hello, Dolly!"

That made the other four elderly people double over with laughter, and start singing the old Broadway song.

Adam explained, "This bunch gets tickled every time they hear someone say it."

"Is Dolly your grandmother?" Jade whispered.

"Oh, no," Adam replied, taking Jade by the hand and leading her to the group. "Dolly's just a friend. She was a famous model when she was young, and knew lots of interesting artists."

"And in what century was that?" Jade asked out of the corner of her mouth.

"In the late nineteen forties, just after World War Two," Adam replied as they went to greet Dolly. "She lived in the south of France, and actually modeled for Picasso and Dalí. She really has an amazing story."

"Let's get the lead out!" the lady named Vivian barked at the group. "Lunchtime will be over before we know it. Hup, two, three, four! Hup, two, three four!"

Vivian marched backward like a drum major, lifting her feet high in quick steps.

Adam chuckled. "Viv is a retired army colonel. Well, not so retired. As you can see, she still likes to order people around."

They met up with the group by the waterfall, and Adam made the introductions. "You've met Dolly, and this is Vivian."

Vivian gave Jade's hand a firm shake. "Put 'er there," Vivian said. "Any friend of Adam's is a friend of mine."

The man in the tweed suit and brass-tipped walking stick was next. He had a severe limp in his right leg and bowed stiffly. "I'm George," he said. "It's a pleasure, my dear."

Jade nodded back to George as Adam whispered, "George was a professor of Art History."

Next in line was a barrel-chested man carrying a pair of camp stools. He set them down and, with a self-conscious tug of his sweater, stepped forward to meet Jade. *"Encantada, señorita,"* he said, flashing a brillant smile. "I am Alberto Martinez, and you are just as lovely as Adam said."

Jade gestured to her faded overalls in embarrassment. "Thanks, Alberto, but this isn't really my best look."

The group parted to reveal a very tall, very thin woman with chocolate-colored skin, and the most wrinkles Jade had ever seen on a human being. "Jade, I'd like you to meet Miss Perkins," Adam said proudly. "Miss Perkins is a nonagenarian."

"Sorry?" Jade said, confused.

Dolly cupped one hand around her mouth and whispered loudly, "That means she's over ninety, dear. Isn't that amazing?"

Miss Perkins took Jade's hand in hers and laid her other hand on top of it. "Adam tells me that you are a musician," she said in a frail voice. "I love music."

Jade smiled. "I play the guitar. Do you play an instrument?"

Alberto answered for Miss Perkins. "She used to play the piano. It was beautiful."

Jade was about to ask why she stopped, but then she noticed Miss Perkins's gnarled hands. It was clear she had arthritis.

Adam clapped his hands together. "Well, now that everyone's met everyone, what do you say we eat? Jade said she's starved, which could be a very scary thing."

Jade slapped playfully at Adam. "That's what I get for being honest."

She helped him get the picnic basket from the bicycle. He'd brought a tablecloth, which they spread on the ground in front of the boulders. Then Adam helped Miss Perkins sit down on one of the camp chairs. Since George had a bad leg, he got the other chair.

Alberto, who was one of the youngest in the group, sat cross-legged on the ground next to Vivian, while Dolly kneeled beside Adam.

"I made chicken salad sandwiches," Adam announced. "I know it's Dolly's and Miss Perkins's favorite. And let's see . . . Alberto's the vegetarian. So I packed you a cheese sandwich." He handed Alberto his sandwich, and then gave George a fruit salad.

"Thank you, Adam." George winked at Jade and added, "I'm watching my figure."

Jade took a sandwich from Adam and a glass of lemonade from Vivian. This was by far the strangest date she'd ever been on. For a fleeting moment the thought occurred to her that maybe she was still sleeping on her couch and this was all just a bizarre dream.

She took a sip of lemonade and asked, "So, how did all of you meet?"

"Hyde Park Manor," Vivian replied. "It really brought us all together."

"Not all of us, Vivie dear," Dolly said, taking a delicate nibble of her sandwich. "We found George at Mountain Meadows."

Jade cocked her head in confusion.

"Hyde Park Manor is a senior residence," Adam said. "So is Mountain Meadows."

"I figured that," Jade said. "But how do you fit into this picture?"

"Oh, he sits at the very center of it," Miss Perkins said. "You see, Adam came to us when he was barely five years old."

"That's when my mother became the receptionist at Hyde Park Manor," Adam explained. "She was only twenty-four when the divorce happened, and couldn't find a job anywhere. She was pretty desperate. Then, an opening came up at Hyde Park Manor. She had to bring me with her to the interview, which is where I met Miss Perkins and Alberto—"

"And don't forget me," Dolly said, with a flourish of her scarf. "I was there too."

Adam chuckled. "No one could forget you, Dolly." He took a sip of lemonade and continued. "Anyway, my mother met some of the residents at the interview, who liked her instantly."

"Adam's mother was charming," Miss Perkins added. "But it was little Adam in his funny derby hat that won our hearts."

Adam tipped his hat to Miss Perkins. "Thank you, Miss P."

Dolly took over the story. "We begged the management to hire Laura—Adam's mother—and we all promised to take care of

Adam while she was at work. Which we did."

Alberto leaned forward. "We took our job very seriously. Miss Perkins made a schedule, and we followed it. Miss Perkins taught him to read, I taught him Spanish—"

Dolly struck a model's pose. "And I introduced him to art, music, and the theater."

Vivian tapped Jade on the knee. "When I moved to Hyde Park Manor a year later, I took over the Phys Ed. We played ball, went for long hikes and, of course, played—"

"Golf," Adam cut in. "Vivian doesn't like to brag, but she was women's champion of the U.S. Army for five years in a row. Toured the U.S. and Europe."

Vivian blushed with pleasure. "Oh, Adam. You don't need to tell Jade that."

Adam draped his arm around Vivian's shoulders. "She's still a terror on the golf course. I have to really push it to keep up with her."

Jade wiped her mouth with the cloth napkin Dolly had given her and said, "So you four are Adam's nannies?"

Miss Perkins laughed. "I suppose we are."

Jade looked at George, who had been silent through most of the story. "What about you, George? How do you fit into this tale?"

"George is our art teacher," Adam explained. "He gave Hyde Park a mission."

"We became artists of the world," Dolly declared.

"Now, now, Dolly," Miss Perkins murmured. "Let George tell his story."

George smoothed his mustache, then began to speak. "Once Adam's nannies—as you call them—decided that he was exhibiting an artistic bent, they set about looking for an art teacher. I had been teaching watercolor at Mountain Meadows, and that's where they recruited me. Soon I had become Adam's full-time art instructor."

"And everyone else's too," Dolly added. "All of us took up watercolor painting."

"When was this?" Jade asked.

Adam shut one eye in thought. "Umm . . . I was ten. So that would be seven years ago."

"Some of you have definitely improved over the years," George said, though Jade noticed he was careful not to mention any names. George leaned in closer toward Jade and confided, "Once these delightful people became my friends, we decided I should leave my previous situation and move into the Manor. And so I did."

Miss Perkins pulled a small bag from her pocket and held it out to Adam. "Chocolate, anyone? Or a cookie?" She pulled another bag from her other pocket. "I also have sugar-free toffee, George."

"Miss Perkins always carries chocolates and cookies in her pockets," Adam whispered loudly to Jade as they passed the little bags of treats around. "She's worried that one day we may get stranded too far from a grocery store and starve to death."

Miss Perkins nodded firmly. "That is correct, Adam. I don't take civilization for granted."

"I adore chocolates," Dolly said, handing the bag to Jade. "At my age I find there are really only two things I'm passionate about: laughter and chocolate."

Jade plucked a chocolate truffle from the bag and popped it in her mouth. "Mmm! Delicious," she murmured. "I think I've just found my passion."

Alberto nudged Adam and said, "Remember that on Valentine's Day, my boy. Chocolates and, of course, roses."

"Red roses!" Dolly clasped her hands to her breast. "My home used to be filled with red roses from all my admirers."

Vivian passed on the chocolates and took two cookies. "I've always been a carnation gal. They smell good and last longer."

Jade couldn't get over how comfortable she felt nibbling chocolate and drinking lemonade with this group of eccentric strangers. It was actually fun. A curious thing was happening too. The more she found out about Adam, the more mysterious he became. She wanted to know more about this unusual boy.

"So, Adam, it sounds like you spend most of your time at Hyde Park Manor," Jade said, pouring another glass of lemonade. "But where do you live?"

Adam gestured to the group. "With my family."

Jade blinked in confusion. "You live in a retirement home?"

"Adam is the youngest resident at Hyde Park Manor," Vivie said. "You see, Adam's mother rose from secretary to manager while Adam was in middle school."

"Then, a few years ago, management decided to sell off the Manor," George said, "which meant we would all have to find a new place to live."

"And Adam's mom would lose her job," Alberto said.

"And we'd lose Adam," Mrs. Perkins said.

"So we all pooled our savings and bought the darn building," Vivian said. "Laura kept her job, and she and Adam moved out of their tiny apartment to a bigger apartment on the third floor."

Jade shook her head. "That's an amazing tale."

Dolly cupped Adam's chin in her hand. "He's an amazing boy."

Adam's nannies took bites of their cookies or chocolates and chewed contentedly, all the while gazing at Adam. Each aged face was filled with unabashed love.

Jade studied Adam's profile. He was leaning back on his elbows, with his feet extended in front of him. In his vest and derby Adam looked like a boy from the 1890s. An extremely hot boy at that!

George pulled out a tiny sketch pad like

the one Adam always carried, and began drawing. While George sketched, Dolly whispered, "Jade? I know you are a musician, but we all were wondering if you had any interest in public art?"

"Art?" Jade whispered back.

The group exchanged meaningful looks. Finally Adam said, "Should we tell her about our project?"

Miss Perkins gave the official nod of approval.

"Where should I begin?" Adam asked.

"Begin at the beginning," Miss Perkins urged. "And when you get to the end, stop."

Adam's eyes twinkled as he spoke. "It started out as a reaction to the city council's decision to keep those ugly buildings by the freeway entrance."

"We all thought they could use a little beautification," Dolly cut in.

Vivian shrugged. "George had been teaching us art for years and we were already a team. We'd done several murals at the Manor."

"So it was a natural leap," Alberto explained, "to go from private art to public."

Jade was thoroughly confused. "You painted a mural?"

Adam nodded eagerly. "We've painted lots of murals. First we did the stars and planets on the warehouse that became the Atomic Café."

"No way!" Jade gasped.

"Then we painted that crumbling drugstore downtown."

"And last week?" Jade whispered in awe. "Ed's parking garage?"

"We did that," Adam said, wiggling his eyebrows.

"You guys are Art Attack?" Jade gasped.

The five senior citizens beamed proudly.

"That's us," George said. He turned his pad to show Jade his sketch. It was a drawing of them all standing in front of their latest mural, which was of a window looking out onto the sea. He'd written the words ART ATTACK in ornate handwriting in the lower-right-hand corner.

Jade was impressed. "My mother's in real estate, and she says your art has actually increased the value of these buildings."

"Well, I certainly hope so," Dolly said. "Art increases the value of everything it touches."

Vivian pulled a newspaper clipping out

of her pocket. It was a photo of a shuttered factory near the riverfront district. "This is our next project. Would you care to join us?"

Jade blinked in surprise. "Me? But I'm not a painter."

Dolly cupped her hand around her mouth and whispered loudly, "Neither is Vivian. That's why she stands guard."

"That's right," Vivian said. "Standing guard is what I do best. I could use another lookout."

Jade looked at Adam, who was watching her reaction. "It might be dangerous," he warned. "It *is* trespassing. Some might even call it defacing other people's property."

She pictured herself sneaking around the streets of Wheaton, spraying gobs of paint on old buildings, and standing lookout with Vivian—and it made her laugh out loud. "It sounds like fun," she declared. "Wicked fun."

"So what do you say?" Dolly asked eagerly. "Are you with us?"

Miss Perkins raised one hand. "Now, Dolly, don't put any pressure on the young lady. Jade will know when the time is right to join us."

Adam was still studying Jade's face

intently, as if searching for something. Then he said, "Miss Perkins is right. Jade will let us know." He clapped his hands as if to change the subject. "In the meantime, I believe you promised you'd play us a tune."

Adam jumped to his feet and brought Jade her guitar. She usually felt a little awkward about playing for people she'd just met, but somehow Jade knew this would be pure fun. She quickly checked to make sure the guitar was in tune. Then she played a tune she was certain everyone would know: "You Are My Sunshine."

They all sang along, clapping their hands. Alberto had a strong baritone voice, and Adam sang harmony. Next she played "Down in the Valley" and "Both Sides Now." Most of them didn't know "Both Sides Now," but they insisted it was wonderful.

"Now play one of your favorites," Adam suggested.

"Okay." Jade smiled at Adam and said, "Normally I just play songs by other people, but today I'll make an exception. This is one that I wrote."

"It would be an honor to hear it," Adam said simply.

If anyone else had said that, it would have sounded corny. But Jade knew he was sincere, and that made it okay. Miss Perkins and the others nodded their agreement.

Jade closed her eyes and chose the song that she had just finished—"Shoot the Moon." She struck a chord and sang the opening lyrics.

"Somewhere in my heart I'm yearning,
Yearning to let you know.
Somewhere in my heart I'm burning,
Burning to just let go."

When Jade's song came to an end, a stillness fell upon the group. Finally Miss Perkins said quietly, "That was lovely, Jade. Simply lovely."

Dolly nodded, wiping a tear away. "Beauty makes me weep. I can't help it."

"I could listen to you all afternoon, my dear," George said. "Thank you."

Jade tucked her pick under the strings on the neck of her guitar. "I'd love to play for you some more, but there's a meeting I have to go to at three."

"Did you say three?" Alberto checked his

pocket watch and frowned. "It's nearly three thirty."

"What?" Jade sprang to her feet. "I have to go. Oh, dear, I really have to go."

"Where do you need to go in such a rush?" Vivian asked.

"I have to meet a boy," Jade said, jumping to her feet. "And I'm late."

"A boy!" Dolly gasped, looking at Adam.

"I mean a *group,*" Jade corrected, seeing the concerned looks on their faces. She crossed her fingers behind her and told a tiny white lie. "A, um, study group."

"Don't worry," Adam said, after conferring with Vivian. "I'll take you there."

Jade quickly tried to put things back in the picnic basket and help clean up, but she was really rattled. One part of her was very upset about being late for her meeting with Zephyr. The other part of her didn't want to leave Adam. It was extremely confusing. For the first time that afternoon she felt awkward and embarrassed in front of Miss Perkins and the others. She suddenly developed a bad case of motor mouth.

"I had a wonderful time, a really wonderful time," she said, grabbing the hand of each one of them and shaking it. "Thank you for the lunch, and I'm sorry I have to go, but I'm late." She looked at Alberto's watch once more. "Oh, dear. I'm really late! And I don't know how I'm going to get there!"

Beep-beep!

Adam honked the horn of the Dodge minivan, which had been parked on the street by Swedenburg Park. "Did someone call for a taxi?" he yelled out the driver's window.

Jade was so flustered that she hadn't even noticed Adam leave to get the car. Now she stood frozen in place while Adam ran to get her guitar and put it in the back of the van. It seemed impolite to just leave them. "Adam, this is really rude," she said to him under her breath. "I feel awful."

Adam looked her straight in the eye and spoke in a voice that only she could hear. "Breathe. Everything is going to be fine. I'll drive you to meet your study group and then come back to get them. Now turn and wave good-bye to my friends. They like you enormously."

Jade did as she was told. She took a deep

breath, plastered a big smile on her face, and turned to wave. "Good-bye, everybody," she called, hopping into the passenger side of the car. "It's been a wonderful afternoon."

Adam accented her good-bye with a couple of honks of the horn, and they pulled away from the curb. Jade leaned her head back against the seat and took another deep breath.

For about a minute Jade felt happy and relaxed as she watched the park disappear in the distance. But when they turned back onto Blake Avenue, she gasped suddenly, "Adam! I can't remember the address. I have no idea where we're going!"

8

Half an hour later, Adam and Jade were still circling the neighborhood around Blake Avenue. Jade knew that the street where Zephyr lived was named after a tree, and she knew his band practiced in a studio in back of the house. But she couldn't remember the house number, or the actual street name.

"Does Ivy qualify as a tree?" Adam asked as they cruised past Ivy Street heading north on Blake Avenue.

"No," Jade moaned. "It's not Ivy. It's not Elm, or Maple or Oak." She shook her head. "Ooh! I can't believe I don't remember the street name."

"Why don't you call this guy?" Adam

asked, turning onto Cincinnati Boulevard, which ran north and south. "Surely he'd know the name of his street."

Jade hadn't called Zephyr on her cell phone because she'd have to do it in front of Adam, and that would be too embarrassing. But she was running out of time. She had to take action. Her cell phone was right in the outside pocket of her guitar bag. Jade started to get it out, then hesitated. She'd have to ask information for Zephyr's number, and then Adam would know exactly who she was going to see. She decided to find a phone booth.

Just then they passed a tiny corner store that had a pay phone out front. Jade was about to tell Adam to stop when he called out, "Sycamore."

"That's it!" Jade yelled. "He lives on Sycamore. Turn!"

"I know this street," Adam said as he turned right onto a street bordered by mature sycamore trees and older homes. "What's the address?"

"I-I don't remember," Jade confessed. "But it's got a little studio in back."

The fourth house on the left had a cottage

in back, and Jade tapped Adam on the shoulder. "Stop here. This could be it."

"Couldn't be," Adam said, without slowing down. "That's Zephyr Strauss's house."

"Stop!" Jade shrieked. "That's who I'm going to see."

Adam slowed down and pulled into an empty driveway. He stopped the car, then turned to look at Jade. "Why didn't you say so? I know Zephyr. I didn't know he belonged to a study group."

"It-it's not a study group, exactly," she stammered. Jade could feel the red crawl up her neck to her face as she realized she'd been caught in her lie. "I just said study group because, well, it was kind of complicated to explain to Miss Perkins and the others. Actually, we *are* studying music. Zephyr asked me to jam with the group today."

Jade could see by his expression that Adam knew Zephyr meant more to her than she'd let on.

"I understand," he said finally. Adam turned the car around, and they rode back to Zephyr's house in silence. Jade felt terrible. She'd told a lie, and now everything felt awkward.

"Adam, thank you for a wonderful picnic," Jade said as she got out of the van. She grabbed her guitar from the back and ran around to his side of the van. "I mean it. I love your family, and your whole weird, wacky life."

A smile crept slowly across Adam's face. Then he touched the tip of her nose with his fingertip. "I've been waiting for the longest time," he murmured. "And suddenly—here you are."

Jade stood on the curb and watched Adam drive away. His words were simple and sweet, and she longed to hear more. Unfortunately, she had a rehearsal to get to, and she was over an hour late.

The band was heavy into the middle of a song called "White Noise" when Jade entered the cottage, which had been converted into a recording studio. The walls were covered with thick layers of sound-proofing foam. Concert posters were taped to every inch of wall space, including the ceiling. One whole wall was lined with posters from classic rock bands like The Who and The Clash, including an auto-graphed photo of Jimi Hendrix. Four guitars hung on hooks from another wall, next to assorted connecting cables and guitar cords.

A mixing console with two computers filled one corner. The band was set up in front of it with Mac Halloway's drum kit at the back, and Zephyr and his bass player, Charlie Riddle, stood at two microphones facing the front door. Stacks of amplifiers created a wall behind each mike, and digital effects boxes were strewn around the guitarists' feet on the carpeted floor.

Jade stood respectfully just inside the door and listened until the band finished their song. Zephyr leaped in the air, doing a perfect windmill swing of his right arm to strike the final chord just as he went down on one knee.

Jade applauded way too enthusiastically. She felt like a dweeb.

When she stopped clapping, Charlie Riddle cracked, "Well, look what the cat dragged in!" He gestured with his thumb to Zephyr, who was engrossed in tuning his guitar. He hadn't looked her way once. "He was starting to worry."

Mac Halloway twirled a drumstick as he

said, "Yeah, Zeph was afraid you'd stood him up."

Jade winced. It really had been a date.

"I'm really sorry, Zephyr," she said. "I had to go to this lunch and then I forgot your address and, well . . ." Jade didn't want to add any more white lies to her list, so she shrugged. "I just screwed up."

"Hey, it's cool," Zephyr said, finally looking at her. He played a sizzling blues riff. "You're here. Now we can do some serious jamming."

"Uh, right." Jade hastily tried to unzip her guitar bag. First the zipper got stuck. Then she knocked herself in the face with the guitar neck as she pulled it free from the bag. Then she held it in the air and groaned, "Oh, no. Wrong guitar."

She'd brought her beatup old acoustic by mistake. There was no way for her to plug in with the band. "I didn't get a chance to go home," she said, giggling nervously. "And now you must think I'm an idiot bringing this thing here."

"Idiot, no," Zephyr said with a chuckle. "Airhead, maybe." He walked over to the row of guitars hanging on the wall and plucked a sleek double cutaway electric guitar with a glossy black enamel finish off its hook. "Here. Try this one."

"A Gibson SG." Jade slipped the guitar strap over her shoulder and slid her hand up and down the neck of the guitar. "Nice feel," she said, with an approving nod.

She hadn't noticed that Zephyr had set up another microphone for her. As she walked toward Zeph's mike, she tripped over her microphone cable. The microphone fell over, and an earsplitting shriek of feedback blasted from the huge Kustom PA speakers. Jade slammed her hands over her ears and cried, "Sorry. Sorry."

While Charlie quickly turned down the volume control on the PA amp, Zephyr righted the microphone.

"I swear to you, I am not always this out of it," Jade said. Try as she might, she couldn't control her nervous giggling. "I think my brain must be oxygen deprived, or something truly terminal like that."

Jade expected the boys in the band to crack a joke, or do something to make her feel more at home—but they didn't. Jade felt like an ant under a giant magnifying glass, and Mac and Charlie were the two boys holding the glass and watching her squirm.

Zephyr patted her on the shoulder. "Jade, relax. We're just hanging out and playing tunes."

If that was true, why did she feel so uncomfortable? Jade remembered Adam's advice and took a deep breath. But it didn't seem to help. Zephyr struck the opening notes for "White Noise," the song the band had just played, and Jade tried to join in, but she was just too nervous. When the lead break came, Zephyr took the first eight bars, then nodded for her to take a solo, but she was too tentative. She could see Charlie rolling his eyes at Mac.

Jade was certain a big L had formed on her forehead, which already felt greasy, since she hadn't taken a shower. Nervous sweat trickled down her sides from her armpits. The more she thought about her greasy hair and forehead and sweaty armpits, the more she wanted to run.

Suddenly a new tune joined the mix. It was the *Barney* theme song: "I love you, you love me." And, horror of horrors, it was coming from the cell phone in her guitar bag. She tried to ignore it, but Charlie and Zephyr stopped playing to figure out where the weird sound was coming from.

"Oh, god! It's my phone." Jade slipped the guitar off her shoulder and tried to lean it against something where it wouldn't fall over. "I'll get it."

She dove for the zipper pocket on her guitar case, explaining, "My brother programmed that tune. As a joke." She yanked the phone out of the case and marched outside the cottage to answer the call. She muttered under her breath as she went, "And I'm going to kill him for it. Then I'm going to kill this caller, and after that, I think I'll kill myself." Jade held the little purple phone to her ear. "What?" she snapped.

There was a long pause. Finally Keesha said, "Jade? Are you okay?"

Her anger instantly disappeared. "Keesha, help! I'm over at Zephyr's house and I have to get out of here!"

"Hold it! Rewind the tape," Keesha cut in. "Did you just say you were at Zephyr's house?"

"Yes!"

"That should be a good thing. I mean, isn't this what you hoped for?"

"No." Jade cupped her hand over the phone and ducked into the hedge as far away from the door as possible. "It's a bad thing. I'm a total waste. I can't sing. I can't play. I'm tripping over things."

"A little awkwardness can be charming."

"Trust me, it's not. Mac and Charlie are staring at me like I'm some kind of psycho-bimbo who just crashed their rehearsal."

"Who cares about them," Keesha said. "What does Zephyr think?"

"I don't know what Zephyr thinks. I never know what he thinks. He's like this big impenetrable wall of cool." She inched back along the cottage wall and peeked in through the window. Zephyr was standing at the mike, playing another solo, his eyes closed and head back. "I mean, he's still in there wailing on that guitar. I'm not sure he knows I'm gone."

"What are you wearing?"

"What kind of question is that?"

"Girl, it's an important question," Keesha replied. "Maybe you've made a bad fashion choice, and that has lessened his interest."

Jade looked down at her overalls. Okay, so this wasn't her get-a-guy outfit, but Zephyr didn't seem to care one way or the other. She watched as he practiced some more stage moves, swinging his arm and jumping high in the air. "I think I could be naked and Zephyr wouldn't notice," she commented.

Keesha whistled softly. "Whoa! That's scary."

"You're telling me," Jade hissed. "Keesha, it's 911 time. Come rescue me!"

"I'll be right over," Keesha said. "As soon as I find my car keys and put on a little makeup."

"Wait!" Jade shouted into the phone. "You don't know where Zephyr lives."

"He's on Sycamore Way," Keesha said.

"How did you know that?" Jade asked.

"Hey! You're not the only girl who's had her eye on that boy," Keesha said. "When I got my driver's license I cruised his house every day for a month."

"What?" Jade gasped. "You never told me that."

"There are a lot of things I've never told you," Keesha replied. "See you in ten minutes."

Jade clicked off her cell phone and tried to summon the courage to go back inside the studio. Playing with Side Effects should have been a dream come true. But it had turned into a nightmare. All she wanted to do now was figure out a graceful way to leave.

The cottage door creaked open, and Zephyr stuck his head outside. "You know, you can come back inside if you want."

Jade stayed where she was in the hedge. "No," she said, with a shake of her head. "I think I'm better off here in the greenery."

Zephyr stepped out on the small porch, letting the screen door swing shut behind him. "We could play something else," he offered.

Jade made a face. "I doubt things would improve. I think I'd better try again some other day."

To her surprise, she saw a look of disappointment cloud his face. "Well, if that's what you want. . . ." He jammed his hands into the pocket of his jeans. "I'm cool with it."

"Thanks, Zeph," Jade said, taking a small step out of the hedge. "If you'll just hand me my guitar and my clown nose, I'll be on my way."

This time Zephyr surprised her by laughing out loud. "That's what I like about you," he said, shaking his head in admiration. "You are one funny lady!"

Jade's jaw dropped open. Just when she thought her chances with Zephyr had been squashed for good, he paid her a compliment. And it had nothing to do with music. This was truly a day for surprises.

9

Keesha finally pulled up to Zephyr's house twenty minutes later in her lime green VW Bug. Jade saw that in her rush to come rescue Jade, Keesha had managed to cruise by Lucy's house and pick her up too. Both girls were anxious to hear all about Jade's day.

Jade climbed in the back and set her guitar on the seat beside her. She leaned back and gathered her thoughts. No way was she going to tell her friends about her picnic with Adam. Lucy might understand, but not Keesha. So Jade confined her story to the disastrous jam session at Zephyr's. She told them how she'd won the Klutz of the Year award by knocking over the microphone, and then bombed out in the music department.

"Here's the worst part," Jade said. "I counted all the words Zephyr said to me from the time I arrived at his house until I left. And they added up to thirty-five."

"Thirty-five!" Keesha sputtered. "I can use that many words in a single sentence."

"I bet you could hit fifty easy if you made the effort," Lucy agreed.

"Hey! Now you're making me sound like some kind of conversation hog," Keesha protested.

Lucy shrugged. "If the shoe fits . . ."

Keesha's jaw dropped open. "Jade? Did you hear that? Lucy just dissed me big-time!"

"Enough about you," Lucy said, turning around in the front seat. "Let's talk about Jade. How are you going to win Zephyr back?"

Jade frowned. "I didn't say I'd *lost* him. I just blew my jam session with the band."

Lucy chewed nervously on her lower lip. "That could count as a major strike against you, since Zephyr's world *does* revolve around music."

"Music!" Keesha cried. "Jade can win him back at the Battle of the Bands."

"Excuse me?" Jade leaned forward between the seats. "I'm not trying to win anyone."

"Hello? What about Truth or Dare?" Keesha challenged. "What about your letter?"

"You may recall that the postman delivered that letter to the wrong person," Jade pointed out, punching the back of Lucy's seat.

Lucy spun. "Look, I told you I was sorry about that. I didn't mean to give it to—what was his name—Ben?"

Jade shook her head. "Adam. Adam Lockhart."

Lucy snapped her fingers. "That's right. Strange cute guy."

"Not so strange," Jade corrected. "Just different. And *extremely* cute."

"What?" With a screech of tires, Keesha swerved the tiny green car over to the curb. She turned off the engine and set the emergency brake. "No way I can drive if you're going to use the words 'extremely cute' about What's-His-Name."

"Adam." Jade crossed her arms defiantly. "His name is Adam."

"Adam, right." Keesha twisted around

in her seat and looked Jade straight in the eye. "Okay, spill."

"There's nothing to spill," Jade said, telling her third lie for the day. It was getting pretty easy for her.

"I see. Did you, or did you not, call Adam and tell him that his Special Delivery letter went to the wrong address?"

"There hasn't been a good time for that call," Jade mumbled.

Keesha narrowed her eyes and studied Jade's face. "I don't think she's giving us the whole story, Lucy. What do you think?"

"Your palm, please." Lucy took hold of Jade's left hand and flipped it over. "I think it's time to use the psychic lie detector."

Jade groaned and tried to pull her hand away. "Oh, no. Not Madame Lucinda. When did you start that—in seventh grade?"

"That's right," Keesha said, peering over Lucy's shoulder at Jade's palm. "She sees all and tells all. And she hasn't done a reading for us in a while."

Lucy squeezed Jade's hand and examined the lines crisscrossing her palm. Then she turned Jade's hand to the side and looked at the lines by her little finger.

"Interesting," Lucy murmured, turning the palm up once more. "Very interesting."

"What do you see?" Jade asked, leaning forward. "Tell me."

"Well, the good news is you're going to be extremely wealthy and very famous," Lucy said.

"Where does it say that?" Keesha demanded. "I don't see any dollar signs."

Lucy pointed to the straight line extending down from the ring finger. "This deep single line that crosses the Mount of the Sun tells us she's going to achieve fame because of her amazing talent."

Keesha squinted at Jade's hand. "That itty-bitty line says that? Awesome."

Lucy wiggled Jade's thumb. "Her thumb is stiff, which tells me that she's a little bit stubborn and a lot secretive."

"Aha!" Keesha cried. "I knew it."

"Hey, my thumb's not stiff," Jade protested. "I can wiggle it. See?" She demonstrated by twirling it. "And I'm not *that* stubborn."

Keesha held up her thumb. "Check mine."

Lucy tested Keesha's thumb. "Um-hmm. Just as I suspected."

"What?" Keesha looked worried.

"Yours is very loose," Lucy announced. "That means you are ruled by impulse."

Keesha put one hand to her chest and batted her eyelashes. "Impulsive? *Moi?*"

Jade chuckled. "You are the most impulsive person I know."

Keesha hid her hand behind her back and said to Lucy, "Tell me more about Jade and all of those secrets she's been keeping from us."

Lucy traced a line from the base of Jade's thumb up toward her fingers. "This line is crossed. That means she is loved by two men."

"Are you serious?" Jade held her palm up to her nose. "Does it really say that, or are you making that part up?"

"Madame Lucinda never makes things up," Lucy said, in her best gypsy accent. "She only tells what she sees."

Jade studied her palm. Could it be possible that both Zephyr and Adam really liked her? She shoved her hand in front of Lucy's face. "Tell me how it all turns out."

Lucy clucked her tongue and shook her

head. "The little cross at the top means not so great."

"We die?" Jade squeaked.

Lucy chuckled. "Of course you don't die. But one of those guys has got to go."

"How do you know that?" Keesha demanded.

"I just know." Lucy put one hand on her hip. "You tell me how many love triangles have happy endings."

Keesha thought about it for a second. "Uh . . . zip?"

"That's right," Lucy said. "Zero. *Nada.*"

"Love triangle," Jade repeated with a gulp. "I think you're making a giant leap here." After all, she'd only had a picnic lunch with Adam, and a pretty humiliating music session with Zephyr.

Lucy studied Jade's palm once more, and her face brightened. "Your fate line, which is this little line that travels from the heel of your palm upward, says that you will find unexpected happiness."

Jade grinned. "I like that."

"You are a visionary," Keesha murmured, shaking her head in admiration at Lucy. "No doubt about it."

Lucy turned Jade's hand to look at her wrist. "And you are a major slob."

"How do you know that?" Jade demanded.

"Look." Lucy pointed to the bright spot of yellow by her beaded bracelet. "You've got a huge glob of mustard right there."

Jade pulled her hand back quickly. "That was from my picnic lunch."

"You had a picnic with Zephyr?" Keesha gasped.

"Not exactly," Jade said, feeling her "secretive" thumb start to tingle. "I, uh, ate before I went to his house."

"Hmm . . ." Keesha stared hard at Jade. "Let me review the palm reading. Jade is secretive and stubborn, and she's stringing along two boys—one of whom will probably not work out." She glanced sideways at Lucy. "We know which mister that's going to be." Then she looked back to Jade. "But what do you care? You are going to be a rich and famous slob!"

"All right!" Jade pumped both fists in the air, slamming them into the roof of the car. "Ouch!"

"Hey, watch the car!" Keesha warned.

"Don't worry, Keesha," Lucy joked. "If she breaks it, she can pay to fix it."

"That's right." Keesha flashed a big smile. "And since you're going to be so rich, you can pay my way into the Battle of the Bands dance."

Jade held her palm up to Keesha. "Talk to the palm. I'm not listening."

Lucy suddenly clutched her stomach. "Did you hear that? My stomach just growled. We have to turn this car around and drive through Cactus Jack's. I'm dying for a garden burger. But don't tell Chris. He's not into fast food at all."

Keesha shook her head. "I'm not going anywhere until Miss Tight Thumbs gives us the 411 on Adam Lockhart."

"So you *do* know his name after all," Jade said pointing accusingly at Keesha. "You were just being . . . impulsive."

"Adam Lockhart has sat behind me in practically every class where the teacher uses alphabetical order to make the seating chart," Keesha replied. She imitated a teacher calling roll: "Keesha Kelly. Adam Lockhart. Sara Long."

Jade slumped down in the backseat. "It's

funny," she said thoughtfully. "I've never had Adam in any of my classes."

Keesha waved her hand. "Well, of course not. He burned through all the required courses in the first two years. Now he only takes electives, like Metal Sculpture and Art."

"What else?" Jade asked, wondering how she was ever going to run into him in the halls if he spent all of his time in the art wing.

Keesha shrugged. "How should I know? And what do you care, anyway? Adam's not the guy for you. You know that. And what's up with that hat?"

When Jade didn't respond immediately, Keesha redirected the conversation. "You and Zephyr are the perfect couple. Right?"

"Right." Jade didn't feel like arguing with Keesha right then. At times Keesha reminded Jade of a force of nature, like a tidal wave or a tornado. Once she made up her mind about something, she simply blew down any opposition.

Plus, Jade wanted to keep her feelings about Adam private. She didn't want Keesha and Lucy trying to put an end to something before it ever had a chance to begin.

"Food!" Lucy moaned from the front seat. "I need food. Now!"

Lucy's pitiful wail of hunger was enough to shake Keesha off the subject of Jade's love life.

"Hang on, Lucy," Keesha cried, revving the engine and pulling back out into traffic with a squeal of tires. "Cactus Jack's, coming up."

They zipped through the drive-through at Cactus Jack's, then took a detour to the mall. Fashion á la Carte was having a sale, and Keesha was already looking for a new outfit to wear to the Battle of the Bands dance. Jade went along for the ride, listening with half an ear as Keesha and Lucy planned what they should do on the night of the dance.

Hours later, when Keesha dropped Jade off in her driveway, Jade spotted something Keesha didn't see. It was a note taped to her front door. The note had been folded into the shape of a bird, so Jade knew instantly who had left it.

She stood in front of the front door, waiting for Keesha and Lucy to drive off. Then she carefully unfolded the little white dove, and read it:

To Whom It May Concern:
1. Ever since our picnic,
    a. I can't stop thinking about you
    b. I can't stop burping (Who made those sandwiches, anyway?)
    c. I stopped thinking and started singing
2. When I dropped you at Zephyr's band practice, I was
    a. proud of you
    b. jealous of Zephyr
    c. thinking of joining the band. Need a tambourine player?
3. I realize we don't know each other. I would like to
    a. change that
    b. see more of you
    c. see lots more of you
4. As a follow-up to item 3, what are you doing
    a. right at this moment?
    b. for the rest of your life?
    c. for lunch on Monday?
Want to go out with me? If you're available, meet me at the parking lot at noon. I'll be driving a blue minivan and wearing a smile.

                                                    Adam

Jade folded the note and slipped it into the pocket of her overalls. She knew she had to talk to Adam and tell him the truth. Maybe she'd see him this one more time, and then she'd 'fess up. After that, whatever happened would be up to fate.

10

The moment the bell rang for lunch on Monday, Jade made a beeline for her locker and dumped her books inside. She felt like some kind of criminal sneaking off this way. Lucy and Keesha were clueless about her date with Adam. It was Jade's secret.

Jade glanced nervously over her shoulder, certain that at any moment Keesha would come screaming down the hall, bellowing, "Tell him the truth. The letter wasn't for him!"

Just as Jade came out of the school, an engine revved in the line of cars next to the curb and she jumped. It sounded like a truck. What if it was Zephyr? How would he feel about her hopping in a car with Adam Lockhart? Would it ruin her chances with him, or with the band?

Jade blew her bangs off her forehead. "Get a grip," she muttered under her breath. "Zephyr is always surrounded by mobs of girls. I can certainly have lunch with one boy."

"What's that you're saying to yourself?" a deep voice said next to her.

"Mr. Cooper!" she yelped to the tall black man next to her. "I didn't see you there."

"I wanted to break the good news to you myself," Mr. Cooper said, sliding his sunglasses to the tip of his nose. "You've been selected to compete as a solo artist in the Battle of the Bands."

"All right!" Jade pumped her arm in the air. "That's awesome."

"It was a no-contest vote," Mr. Cooper confided. "That demo tape of yours was right on. Stop by the music room later today and I'll give you your time slot." He gave her a high five and strolled back toward the school.

There's no doubt about it, Jade thought

as she watched her teacher walk away. Mr. C was the King of Cool. "And I am psyched!" she cried, holding her fists above her head.

That was the perfect moment for Adam to pull his minivan up to the curb. He rolled down the window and said, "Let me guess— I'm king of the world, right?"

Jade looked at him in confusion.

"From the movie *Titanic*," Adam explained. "Leonardo DiCaprio raises his hands and shouts, 'I'm king of the world!'"

Jade threw her head back and laughed. "That's how I feel. Adam, I've got awesome news! I've been chosen for the Battle of the Bands."

"Congratulations! This calls for a celebration." Adam reached across the seat and pushed open the passenger door. "Hop in."

Jade jumped into the minivan and didn't waste a second worrying about what anybody might think. She didn't care anymore if Lucy or Keesha, or even Zephyr, saw her. She was floating on Cloud Nine, and nobody was going to take that away from her!

Adam drove them out of the residential district around the high school, into downtown Wheaton. As he turned the minivan onto Calumet Avenue toward Hyde Park, she watched him quietly. She was getting used to his outfits—crisp white shirt, dark tie, and derby. Today he'd added a vest, which made him look unusually attractive.

Jade thought about her situation with Adam and the note. She knew this was the time she was supposed to tell Adam the truth. But he was so sweet . . . and sensitive. How could she hurt him? What if he never found out the note wasn't written for him?

As Jade continued to mull the situation over, they pulled up in front of a weathered but elegant limestone building. The facade was a series of three arched windows, with the front door set in the center arch. Little statues of Greek gods and goddesses filled the niches set between the arches. It was very charming but very old-fashioned.

"Welcome to Hyde Park Manor," he said, leading her into the lobby. "Which is a grand name for a pretty drafty old place."

Jade felt like she had taken a giant step back in time. The carpet, which was badly worn in some places, was a deep burgundy color with a rich paisley pattern. The walls were covered with dark walnut panels, which gave the brass light fixtures a warm glow. An ornate reception desk stood across from the elevator. Behind the desk the wall was filled with wooden cubbyholes, each labeled with a resident's name. Some of the cubbies were overflowing with magazines and letters. Thick ferns in copper buckets were placed strategically around the lobby.

Adam pushed through a swinging half-door into the reception area and tapped the bell on the desk. "This is where I work," he said. "Every afternoon from three thirty to six P.M."

"Are you the bellhop?" Jade asked, running her hands across the elaborate coat of arms emblazoned on the elevator door. "Or the doorman?"

Adam slipped on the maroon uniform jacket that hung on a wooden coat tree just behind the desk. It had gold epaulets and braided trim around the cuffs. He struck a pose and said, "I'm the bellhop, doorman, receptionist, phone operator, plumber and, if need be, pizza dude." Then he slipped the jacket back off and hung it up again. "But today, I am just Adam Lockhart, a guy with a mission: lunch."

Adam hopped over the top of the desk and hit the CALL button next to the elevator. He grinned at Jade. "Are you ready for a treat?"

Jade smiled. "I'm always ready for treats."

"Then let's take the Wonkavator up to the rooftop dining room," Adam said.

As if on cue, the elevator made a "ding" sound, and the doors slid open. They hopped inside, and Adam tapped the button marked 5.

As the elevator rumbled upward, Adam leaned easily against the wall, smiling at her. Jade leaned against the opposite wall, and grinned back. One thing was for certain: A date with Adam was always an adventure.

When the elevator doors opened, Adam explained, "We've now reached the top floor of Hyde Park Manor." He gestured across the narrow hall, where two apartment doors with the numbers 5A and 5B could be seen. "This is where George and Dolly live. They've got the two penthouse apartments."

"Penthouse? Sounds ritzy," Jade remarked.

"Maybe on Fifth Avenue in New York City, but here at the Hyde Park Manor in

Wheaton, Ohio, 'penthouse' just means the top floor. Come on." Adam took Jade by the hand and led her through a heavy metal door to the left of the elevator. It had a stenciled sign on it that read, THIS WAY TO THE ROOF. In smaller letters was another sign beneath it that read, CAUTION: DOORS LOCK AUTO-MATICALLY BEHIND YOU.

"Don't worry," Adam said. "I've got a key."

They continued to hold hands as they climbed the stairs to the roof. Jade had to admit she liked holding Adam's hand.

They stepped through another iron door onto the roof. It was surfaced with asphalt and tar paper. There were four tall brick chimneys, with old TV antennas sprouting out of them like weeds. Most of the antennas had been broken off by the wind. Strips of metal and antenna cable dangled off the chimney sides. The outer wall of the building came up about three feet above the floor to make a protective railing around the roof. At each corner of the building were stone gargoyles that looked like bizarre birds of prey perched on the walls.

Sitting in the center of all the heat vents and antennas was a card table draped with an old-fashioned flowered tablecloth. Little-kid lunch boxes had been set at both place settings.

"Adam!" Jade clapped her hands together. "Did you do this?"

"Dinner for two," he announced.

Jade hurried to examine the lunch boxes. "Can I have the Batman lunch box?"

"But of course," Adam answered in a French accent. He pulled out her chair. "Any-zing for zee mademoiselle."

"Merci beaucoup," Jade answered, in her best French. *"Vous êtes un vrai gentil homme."*

"Whatever you say," Adam quipped. With a flick of his wrist he snapped a red-and-white-checked napkin open and draped it across her lap. Then he pulled out his chair and sat down. "See what a great guy I am?" he said, flipping open his shiny plastic lunch box. "I'm not mentioning a word about you getting Batman and me getting Barbie."

"I've never been much of a Barbie girl," she admitted. "While my friends played with dolls, I played with my Ninja Turtle action figures."

Adam snapped his fingers. "I should

have guessed that. But my choices were limited—Barbie, or the Incredible Hulk. And big green guys worry me."

"Wimp!" Jade teased as she peered inside her lunch box. There was an apple, a peanut butter and jelly sandwich, a bag of corn chips, and a carton of milk. "Total comfort food," she murmured. "Perfect."

"It reminds me of those carefree days in elementary school," Adam said, taking a sip of milk. "Where the only thing you worried about was being first on the swings, or being picked last for kickball."

Jade took a bite of her sandwich and chewed thoughtfully. "So what worries you now?"

Adam answered without hesitating. He ticked off his answers on one hand. "Global warming, world peace, my Art History class, and you." Then he bit into his apple and chewed for a few moments. "Of course you're not really a worry. More a preoccupier of my thoughts."

"Is 'preoccupier' a real word?" Jade asked, giggling.

"Of course," Adam answered with a straight face. "It's right there in the dictionary, along with those other great descriptive words, like 'fantabulous' and 'scrumdiddli-umptious.'"

Jade took a bite of her apple. "I guess I worry about the future. You know, making the right decisions and all." She didn't real-ize until she'd said it that she was talking not just about college and career but about her romantic life too.

"I always say, think big. Shoot for the moon," Adam said as he tipped his chair back and leaned against the air-conditioner duct.

Jade stopped chewing. Those were almost the same words she'd painted on her rock on Signature Hill. She wondered what "Madame Lucinda" would have to say about that.

"That's what I try to do," Adam added.

Jade nodded, smoothing the folds of her napkin in her lap. "It's not always easy."

Adam let his chair flop forward. "Miss Perkins always says nothing worth doing is easy."

"Miss Perkins," Jade repeated. "Where is she, anyway? Hyde Park Manor looks deserted."

Adam leaped out of his chair. "I'm glad you reminded me." He ran to the gargoyle rainspout perched on the north corner of the roof. "Come over here and I'll show you the gang."

A telescope was set up on a tripod next to the gargoyle. Jade hadn't even noticed it when she arrived on the roof. Adam peered through the eyepiece, fiddled with the focusing knob a little, and gave Jade a look. "Over there. See anything?"

Jade closed one eye and peered through the lens with the other. "I see cars and the old Woolworth's building."

"Remarkable," Adam drawled. "Anything else?"

"People. Old people," she added. "In the parking lot in front of the Woolworth's."

"Any of them look familiar?"

"There's George. I recognize his cane. And Miss Perkins. She's so tall and thin. And Alberto and Dolly. They're carrying something. Like . . . buckets."

"What about Vivian?" Adam asked. "Where is she?"

"On the corner. Standing lookout." Jade raised her head and gasped. "Art Attack. They're doing another mural."

"I know nothing," Adam said, holding up his hands in mock innocence. "As far as

I'm concerned, they just went for a painting class in the park."

"In the parking lot, is more like it." Jade peered back through the telescope. "I can't believe it. They're working in broad daylight."

"They have to," Adam said with a grin. "How are a bunch of elderly artists going to see in the dark?"

"With a Seeing Eye dog," Jade cracked. "He could bark whenever they colored outside the lines."

Adam chuckled as he turned the telescope in another direction. "Check this out. It's our first masterpiece."

Jade peered through the telescope again. At first she thought Adam had made a mistake, because she found herself looking at a beautiful stand of birches in full fall foliage. Delicate golden leaves were dropping all around and covering the forest ground. It took her a second to realize that the falling leaves weren't moving. The mural was unbelievably realistic. "That is so cool," Jade murmured.

"Now look to the east," Adam said, turning Jade's shoulders to the right. Near the freeway was the Red Top Brewery building, which had been abandoned for years. Painted on its brick walls were rows of windows bordered with curtains, and sills with flowerpots and cats. "That was Dolly's idea. She likes windows."

Jade turned the telescope slowly in a circle. She saw the moon and stars on the Atomic Café, a flower garden on the side of a garage, and a lake full of bobbing sailboats on the side of a supermarket. Everywhere she looked a huge painting smiled back at her. "Adam! I can see all the murals from here. It's like a giant art gallery."

Adam touched his nose and pointed at her. "That's exactly what Dolly calls it. The Hyde Park Art Gallery."

Jade folded her arms and leaned on the roof wall, taking in the view. "Our town actually looks beautiful!"

Adam leaned on the wall beside her, resting his chin on his folded arms. "I could stay here all day, but we've got to go back." He tapped the face of his watch. "Wheaton High beckons."

They packed up their lunch boxes, and Adam drove them back to school. As they came down Ohio Avenue, they passed

Harpo's restaurant and Jade put her hands on the dashboard. "Turn here!" she ordered. "Turn!"

Adam whipped a right onto Bramble Lane. "Where to next, madam?" he asked, not blinking an eyelash.

"The gnomes. Let's go see how Doc's doing," Jade said. She pushed up the sleeve on his starched white shirt to check his watch. "See? We've got time."

Adam parked a few houses down from the little yellow cottage. "Don't want to be too obvious," he explained. Then the two of them strolled nonchalantly up the street. When they were certain no one was watching, they scurried up the driveway to the little wooded glen behind the cottage. Jade got there first.

"Adam! Look!" she whispered as she knelt at the edge of the grove. "Doc's moved!"

The little ceramic gnome with the glasses was no longer standing by the stream. He had moved next to the bronze statue of the girl sitting on the bench.

Adam knelt beside Jade. "He's spent all these years admiring Snow White from a distance," he whispered. "And now he's finally found his courage to speak to her."

"What's he saying?" Jade asked.

"Let's see . . ." Adam stroked his chin and put on a deep "Doc" voice. "Miss White, I know you have a lot of admirers and I'm just one of seven, but there's a big dance coming up at my school and I would be so very pleased if you would go with me."

"A dance, huh?" Jade tilted her head to look at Adam. "And what does Snow White say to this question?"

Adam turned to face her. "She says, 'I'd love to go with you. And after I win the Battle of the Bands, I'm yours.'"

Jade raised an eyebrow. "Snow White is pretty cocky."

Adam shrugged. "She has a right to be. She's talented, beautiful . . . and did I mention talented?"

There was a rustling in the trees, and Jade and Adam ducked behind the fence. "Do you think Doc heard us?" Jade whispered.

"I don't think he cares," Adam said, peeking through the slats of the fence. "He's too nervous. Snow White still hasn't answered his question."

Jade took a deep breath. The Battle of the Bands was only a few days away. She hadn't even thought of it as a dance. She'd been too preoccupied about *playing* in it. "Snow White needs some time to think about her answer," she said. "She might be too nervous about the competition to go on an actual date."

Adam nodded. Then he took her hand and said, "Then Doc would like to revise his question. How would Miss White like to go on a painting expedition on Wednesday? Say, about four?"

Jade's answer was barely a whisper. "Miss White would love that."

"Doc is happy," Adam whispered back.

The two of them seemed frozen in place, mirroring the two statues in the little garden. Jade could barely catch her breath. Adam's face was only inches from hers, and the only thought going through her mind was the question, Why don't you kiss me?

Adam leaned forward, and Jade closed her eyes, waiting.

"Ba-roo!" The sudden howl of a beagle from the other side of the fence was like an explosion. They both screamed and fell backward. This set the dog off on a mad frenzy of barking.

They scrambled away from the fence, clutching their sides with laughter. Jade and Adam got in the minivan and hurried back to school. But every few seconds they'd burst into laughter again, remembering the sudden appearance of the Hound of the Baskervilles at the fence.

It would have been a perfect date if it hadn't been for the figure in red waiting for them as they pulled into the school parking lot.

11

"Where have you been?" Keesha barked as she marched up to Jade's side of the minivan.

Jade ignored the question. "You know Keesha, don't you?" she said to Adam. "She's been voted the Queen of Rude by the entire student body."

"Sorry, Adam," Keesha apologized as she reached across Jade and high-fived him. "I'm feeling a little hyper today. How's it going?"

"Life is great," Adam replied.

Lucy suddenly squeezed next to Keesha and popped her head through the window. "Hi, Adam. You know me—I'm Lucy."

"Sure I know you," Adam said, tipping

his hat. "Lucy in the Sky with Diamonds," he added, quoting the old Beatles song.

Lucy's face lit up. "My parents named me after that song. Did you know that?"

Adam shrugged. "Lucky guess."

"That's awesome," Lucy said, and giggled.

Keesha pulled open the car door and went straight back into her rant. "For the last fifty-five minutes Lucy and I have torn this school apart looking for you. Where did you go?"

As Jade hopped out of the van, she said in a matter-of-fact tone, "Adam and I went to lunch."

"Oh?" Keesha raised her eyebrows meaningfully. She lowered her voice and whispered, "Did you tell him?"

"I did not," Jade said, cutting her off firmly. She shut the van door and changed the subject. "So, why the big freak-out?"

"Well, while you were doing your disappearing act, Zephyr was trying to find you," Keesha explained.

"Zephyr?" Jade glanced nervously at Adam, who was coming around the side of the minivan. "What does he want?"

"He wants you to join Side Effects."

Jade's eyes widened in shock. "No way!"

Keesha nodded. "Way."

"Is that a good thing?" Adam asked. He eyed Jade carefully to see her reaction.

"Duh!" Keesha put her hands on her hips and wobbled her head. "Side Effects is only the hottest band in Wheaton."

"I know that," Adam said. "But a case could be made for Jade going it alone. She's good enough."

Keesha sighed in exasperation. "If Jade wants to get picked for the Battle of the Bands, she's going to have to—"

"I've *been* picked," Jade said, putting her hand over her friend's mouth. "Mr. C gave me the news just before lunch."

"What?" Keesha cried. "Oh, Jade, that's fantastic!" She wrapped her arms around Jade in a big bear hug.

"Awesome!" Lucy threw her arms around Jade too. Then Lucy and Keesha danced around Jade in a circle, chanting, "She's a winner, I know her, she's a winner!"

"I think your friends need to get out more," Adam cracked. "They're just too shy."

Jade laughed happily. Her friends did

look a bit nutty, with Keesha in her high-fashion heels and tight mini, and Lucy in her patchwork skirt and velvet vest, dancing together in the parking lot.

Keesha suddenly stopped still. "What are you going to do about Zephyr's offer to join his band?"

Jade shook her head. "I think you're making a big leap. The guy hasn't even talked to me since my oh-so-impressive jam session with his band."

"Hey, I heard it direct from the Klingons, who got it straight from Charlie Riddle," Keesha said.

"Klingons?" Adam repeated.

"That's what Keesha calls Zan Teal and Morgan Fifer," Lucy explained. "They're Side Effects' little groupies."

"Good name," Adam said, chuckling.

"So what are you going to say when he asks you?" Keesha persisted.

Jade didn't know. She looked at Adam helplessly. "I'm just wondering why Side Effects would want me."

"Aside from the fact that you're a brilliant musician and songwriter?" Adam grinned, revealing a dimple in his right cheek. "Maybe

Zephyr's a little worried about the vote on Friday night. His group has won twice, but will they win a third time?" Adam shrugged. "Maybe not. Maybe people are tired of hearing the same old 'Big Trouble Ahead' song. Zeph's always said he could use some good harmonies."

Jade blinked in surprise. "He told you that?"

Adam nodded. "Sure. We're old friends. Since middle school."

Jade didn't know why she was so surprised. Of course she knew Adam would have other friends his own age. It just never occurred to her that Zephyr might be one of them.

"I even designed the band's logo," Adam added. "So I know Zephyr's music pretty well. It's not hard to guess why he'd want you to join him."

Lucy nodded. "If Zephyr puts Jade in his band, they'll be fresh and exciting—and will win for sure."

"Brilliant deduction, Watson!" Adam said, pointing to Lucy. "Side Effects *needs* Jade."

Keesha put her hand on her hip. "Is that such a bad thing? Zephyr and Jade were hot when they sang together at the Atomic Café. Everyone could see it."

"But Jade is great as a solo act, too," Lucy cut in.

As her three friends discussed what she should do, Jade shut her eyes and tried to think. Her head was swirling. Since she'd started writing songs, she'd never thought of joining someone else's band. She'd always thought of herself as a solo artist. On the other hand, she and Zephyr *did* sound good together. But it was too big of a decision to make on the spot.

Luckily, the buzzer rang announcing the end of lunch period. The four of them hurried back into the school. Just before they split up to go to their separate classes, Jade thanked Adam for lunch and promised she'd be ready at four on Wednesday. Adam was going to pick her up.

"If I don't see you before," she called, backing away down the hall.

"I look forward to it!" Adam called back in his funny, formal way.

As Jade waved good-bye, Keesha fell in beside Adam and said, "I'll walk with you to Art class."

Mr. C was already at the piano analyzing another tricky chord progression when Jade arrived for Music Theory. Usually Zephyr would have been in the huddle around the piano, but he was clearly waiting for her. "Can I talk to you for a moment?" he whispered as she stepped into the room.

"Sure." Jade tried to sound casual, but she could feel the jolt of adrenaline shooting through her body.

Zephyr took her by the elbow and guided her to the back of the room. He found a secluded spot between some kettledrums wrapped in their black covers and a xylophone.

Jade looked back over her shoulder at the class. Zan Teal and Morgan Fifer were watching Zephyr's every move, clearly jealous of the personal attention he was giving Jade.

"Mr. C gave me the running order for the Battle of the Bands on Friday night," Zephyr said, unfolding a piece of paper. "See, he's got us in back-to-back slots, right at the end of the show." He pointed to Jade's name written next to 7:30, with Side Effects just below at 7:45. "You go on right after the Phreeze," Zeph added.

"You mean, that hot band from Cincinnati?"

Zephyr nodded. "It's a tough draw for you, I know. Those guys are bank. They're going to be a hard act to follow."

Jade grimaced at the thought of having to play right after the Phreeze, who were a high-energy crowd pleaser.

"That's why I wanted to talk to you," Zephyr said. "Seeing the lineup gave me an idea." He cleared his throat awkwardly. "I know it's kind of late notice, but I was thinking—if you joined Side Effects, we would really kick it. The Phreeze wouldn't have a chance."

Jade was too overwhelmed to say anything.

"I mean, we sounded pretty good at the Atomic Café Saturday," Zephyr added. "Seems a shame not to take advantage of it. I think you'll bring something new and fresh to our sound. So what do you think?"

Her smile stretched from ear to ear. Adam was right! Side Effects *did* need her. Zephyr was actually trying to talk her into joining his band.

"Zephyr, that is an awesome offer," she gushed. "I-I'm really flattered."

But something stopped Jade from saying yes outright. She stared at the floor, remembering how Adam and Lucy had encouraged her to go solo.

"All right, people, find a seat," Mr. Cooper's voice called from the piano. "I want you to wrap your little minds around this complex polyrhythm from West Africa. We're going to break it down, and then write it out in standard notation."

"Think about it," Zephyr whispered. "We'll talk about it after class."

Jade couldn't concentrate on a thing Mr. Cooper said. She held her notation book in her lap and dutifully made little x's in it as she wrote out the drumbeat. But her mind was elsewhere. She thought about how she'd felt when she got her first guitar, a cheap Strat knockoff with action so high, it took all the strength in her fingers to press down the strings. How her mom had turned the garage into a studio just so Jade could practice whenever she wanted to.

She thought about the countless hours she'd stood in front of the mirror, practicing her rock 'n' roll sneer, wearing an Avril Lavigne tie. Or spraying her hair platinum blond to look like Gwen Stefani. She remembered how her brother always made her play for his friends when they came over to the house. And even her sister, who was a real prig, had said she liked Jade's style.

Now, when she finally was given a chance to really shine, it was hard to think of sharing the spotlight with a group. Especially the best-known band in the area. She really wanted the chance to see if she could make it on her own, just Jade and the audience.

Before she knew it, class was over. Once again, Zephyr was waiting for her by the door. Behind him in the hallway hovered his two Klingons, Morgan and Zan, waiting to walk him to the water fountain or bathroom, or wherever.

"So?" Zephyr asked. "Did you think about it?"

"I did," Jade replied. "And I'm totally psyched to play with you guys sometime." She took a deep breath. "But not this time. Friday night I'd like to go solo, just to see if I can do it."

"There's no question that you can do it," Zephyr said, shaking his hair out of his eyes.

"But, hey, it's cool. Maybe another time."

Jade shoved her hands in the pockets of her frayed jeans and nodded. Zephyr had his hands in his pockets too. He nodded back. Finally Jade rocked back on her heels and started to leave. "Well . . . I guess we'd better go," she murmured.

Zephyr caught hold of her arm. "Uh, one more thing. About Friday. We don't have to play together, that's cool. But would you like to go with me? As my date?"

Jade froze, her leg raised mid-stride. For three years she'd dreamed of this moment— more than three, if she counted the summer before freshman year. And now that Zephyr Strauss, the object of her affection, had finally asked her out, she felt . . . nothing.

She had to face it. Zephyr was a wonderful musician, and a pretty cool guy. But did her heart beat faster when she saw him? No. Was he fun, or even funny? Not really. Did she want to date him? No.

That final answer was like a lightbulb coming on in her brain.

Jade didn't know how long she'd stood there without responding. Finally Zephyr waved his hand in front of her face. "Yo,

Jade! It's no big deal if you don't want to go out with me."

"It-it's not that I don't want to go with you," she stammered. "It's just that—"

"There's another guy," he finished for her. He bent forward and peered in her eyes. "Yeah, I can see it. Right there."

Suddenly everything was very clear. There *was* another guy. And that guy was Adam. "There *is* someone," she said finally. "There is!"

"My loss. His gain," Zephyr said with a shrug. "But, hey, if we're going to make music together, maybe it's better to keep things on a 'just friends' level."

Jade smiled gratefully. "I'm glad you see it that way." All the confusion was finally gone from her brain. She knew what she wanted, and *who* she wanted!

"Listen, Zeph, I'll see you on Friday night," Jade said as she walked toward the door. "And after that, if you still want me in the band, we'll talk!"

Now that everything was clear, Jade couldn't wait to see Adam. She wanted to tell him about her decision to go solo in the Battle of the Bands. She knew he'd be totally behind her choice. Certainly more than Keesha, who would probably freak out.

After school, she raced out of the building, hoping to catch Adam before he went home. She was one of the first people out the doors, but his minivan was already gone.

Jade stood on the curb for a moment, wondering how he had managed to beat her to the parking lot. Then she shrugged. Her good news could wait. She'd call Adam tonight. And if she didn't reach him today, she'd see him for sure on their big date on Wednesday.

"Whoo-hoo!" Jade played air guitar, kicking her leg out in front of her. "Life is good!"

12

At four o'clock on Wednesday, Jade stood at the picture window in her living room and watched the cars drive down the street in front of her house. Adam's van was nowhere to be seen, but that didn't bother her. Knowing him, he would probably show up on a bike, or in a golf cart. She smiled at the thought of him. With Adam Lockhart, life was one big surprise. She hadn't seen or talked to him since their lunch on Monday, but she was sure he'd bring something fun like flowers or balloons.

Jade impatiently switched her weight from one foot to the other. She pulled her watch with the broken strap out of her backpack and checked the time. Adam had said he'd be there at four o'clock, and it was already four thirty.

"Mom!" she shouted toward the kitchen, where her mother was poring over the new MLS real estate listings for September. "My watch is fast. What time is it?"

Her mother didn't answer, as usual. She was too preoccupied. But April's voice pierced the air. "Four thirty-five, to be exact. And when are you going to get a new watch? That one hasn't worked since you dropped it in the bathtub."

Jade rolled her eyes. Leave it to her sister to use a simple question like "What time is it?" as an excuse for some kind of uptight lecture. "Thank you, Miss Perfect," Jade called.

"You're welcome," April replied. She didn't even react to the Miss Perfect comment. Probably because she thought the title was appropriate.

Jade paced in a circle, over and over. Her brother, Nick, was in his usual place on the couch, studying with his earbud headphones on. "Sit down," he finally shouted. "You're making me nervous."

Jade lifted one of his earbuds and asked, "Did Adam call for me?"

"Nope," Nick replied. "No calls from Adam. Keesha called. She said she'd call back or drop by."

Jade put one hand on her hips. "Why didn't you tell me?"

"You didn't ask." He pressed his earbud back in his ear and continued to bob his head in time to the music.

Jade puffed out her lips in exasperation—which made her think of her makeup. Maybe she needed to apply a little more lip gloss. She hurried back to her room, checking her reflection in the hall mirror for the gazillionth time.

Maybe her clothes weren't right. The last time she had met the Hyde Park Manor brigade, she had worn a pair of overalls. Today she wanted them to see her "fem" side, so she'd put on a black tee, and a flippy cheerleader skirt over red tights, with black socks rolled down over her Doc Martens. Her magenta hair hung straight past her shoulders. She stared at her reflection critically. Hmm . . . was this too girly for Art Attack? After all, the plan was to do some major painting, not make a fashion statement.

"April!" She dove into her closet to find something that would serve as a painter's jacket to wear over her outfit. She hurled clothes from the bottom of her closet onto her bed. "What time is it now?"

April didn't skip a beat. "5:05, and counting," she called from her desk.

"Five?" Jade paused in mid-hurl. "Adam is an hour late. That is too weird." She stepped over the pile that had formed on the floor and went to the kitchen. "Mom! Have you talked to Adam today?" she asked, using her hand to block the page of the real estate book so she could get her mother's full attention.

Kit Chandler looked over the reading glasses perched on her nose. "Adam? The slapjack dealer?"

"Yes!" Jade huffed. "*That* Adam. What other Adam is there?"

"No." Her mom shook her head. "Adam has definitely not called. Today, or any other day."

Jade slumped her shoulder against the refrigerator. Adam hadn't called ever? That, too, seemed odd. She hadn't seen him at school, and he hadn't called. What was going on? They'd had fun on Monday at lunch. Okay, Keesha was a bit rude when they'd returned from lunch, but she'd gotten over herself. And when they'd parted, Adam had said, "I'll see you Wednesday, if not before."

Jade's mother took off her glasses and focused on her daughter. "Is something wrong?"

Jade shook her head slowly. "I'm not sure." She picked up the kitchen phone. "But I'm going to find out."

She dialed information to get Adam's number, and then punched it in. After several rings a woman's voice answered.

"Hello, this is Jade Chandler," Jade said.

"Yes, I know," the woman replied. "I have Caller ID."

Jade couldn't help chuckling. Like mother, like son. "Is Adam there?" Jade asked. "We were supposed to meet today. We had a, um, date."

"I thought that was called off," Adam's mother replied stiffly. "Adam is out with George and the others."

Jade was confused. "But I was supposed to go with him—I mean, them."

"No, I don't think so," Ms. Lockhart replied.

"Well . . . will you tell Adam I called?" Jade asked weakly.

"I'll give Adam the message." His mother hung up without saying good-bye.

Jade was still clutching the phone when she turned back to her mother. "Something weird is definitely going down. But I don't know what."

"Knock-knock! Who's home?" a voice called from the front of the house.

Before Jade or her mother could reply, Keesha strutted into the kitchen in tight jeans and high-heeled boots. She was talking a mile a minute. "I was just at the mall and everything at Fashion Express is, like, thirty percent off, and I thought, Hey, Jade could use some kind of hot outfit for the Battle of the Bands, so . . . here I am. Ready to go back and shop till we drop!"

Jade stared at Keesha for a long time. Then she said, "I don't feel like shopping."

"She's been stood up," her mother explained.

"Mom!" Jade gasped, slamming the phone back on its base. "I never said that. I told you something was weird, that's all."

"That would mean there was some kind of date that I didn't know about." Keesha folded her arms across her chest and walked slowly toward Jade. "Did Zephyr stand you up?"

Jade made a face. "Zephyr? Get real."

Mrs. Chandler slipped her glasses back on her nose and picked up the MLS real estate listings. "Adam is the culprit. He was supposed to be here an hour ago."

Keesha cocked her head. "Adam? You had a date with Adam?"

"Yes!" Jade shouted in exasperation. "What about it?"

Keesha shook her head. "Man, that boy has some kind of nerve asking you out after our conversation on Monday."

Jade's eyes widened in horror. "Keesha! What did you say to him?"

"I told him the truth about the letter mix-up," Keesha said with a shrug. "I knew you'd never get the courage to do it. I felt bad for the guy. It was like you were stringing him along."

"Oh . . . my . . . god." Jade sat down heavily in one of the kitchen chairs.

"What?" Keesha looked confused. "Isn't that what you wanted? For him to know?"

"No!" Jade shot back. "It's what *you* wanted." She put her head in her hands. "I can't believe you'd do something like that without talking to me. Poor Adam."

Keesha's brassy confidence melted away. "I-I thought I was helping. I mean, Zephyr wanted you to be in his band, and here was this guy telling you to go solo—"

"I *am* going solo," Jade cut in. "And it's *my* decision. Not yours. Just like picking my boyfriends is *my* decision." Every time Jade said the word "my," she banged her fist on the table.

"Jade never told me she was into Adam," Keesha tried to explain to Mrs. Chandler. "I-I thought she liked Zephyr, so . . ." Her voice trailed off, and she slumped down in the chair next to Jade. "Okay. I screwed up. Big-time."

"Now what do I do?" Jade groaned.

Mrs. Chandler stood up and poured herself a cup of coffee. "I don't know anything about a letter, or a boy named Zephyr, but what I *do* know is that telling the truth is always best."

"That's right!" Keesha nudged Jade's shoulder enthusiastically. "Call Adam and tell him I made the whole thing up just to get you to go with Zephyr."

"Keesha!" Jade said, swatting at her friend's hand. "Where is your brain? You've been all 'tell Adam the truth,' and now you want me to lie to him again?"

"Okay. You're right." Keesha crossed the room to the phone. "I'll call him and explain the whole situation."

Jade leaped to her feet. "No, this should come from me."

Keesha held out the phone. "So do it."

Jade took the phone and set it back on its cradle. "I already called him. He's not there. And from the sound of his mother's voice, I don't think she wants to talk to me ever again."

Mrs. Chandler took a sip of her coffee. "Well, you have one more option," she said. "Go find Adam. It's always better to deliver the truth face-to-face."

Keesha was already at the door. "I'll drive. I got you into this mess, and I'm going to get you out."

Jade hesitated. "I hope you know I'd like to strangle you right now. Even though this is half my fault. . . ."

"Duh," Keesha said, waggling her head. "I'm not an idiot. I also know that you don't have a car, and the only way you're going to find Adam is if I drive or if your brother lends you his Jeep."

Jade knew the Jeep option was out. Nick had a class. Her mom's car was in the shop. She had no other choice but to go with Keesha. She grabbed her bag. As Jade led Keesha down the hall to the front door, she made a general announcement: "If Adam Lockhart calls this house, give him my cell phone number and tell him to call me immediately. Everybody got that?"

April answered from her room down the hall. "Got it."

Jade and Keesha spent the rest of the afternoon searching for Adam. After a visit to Hyde Park Manor, which seemed to be totally deserted, they stopped at the drugstore wall downtown. That mural had been completed on Monday. Jade knew the group had chosen a new building for their next "Art Attack," but she didn't know which one. She also knew it probably faced Hyde Park Manor, but that didn't narrow the field by much. The only good thing about the search was that Keesha began to be more appreciative of Adam.

"If he's designing these murals," she said to Jade after they had cruised by the four walls that had already been painted, "then this boy is one hot artist."

Jade told Keesha all about her first meeting with Adam, and their walk through the alley and their visit to Bramble Lane. Then she described the picnic at Swedenburg Park and meeting his friends from Hyde Park Manor. Keesha loved hearing about the bicycle built for two. "Sweet!" she said, nodding her approval.

Jade leaned her head against the seat and described their romantic lunch Monday on the rooftop overlooking the Ohio River and the town of Wheaton. "Adam is fun," she explained. "And impulsive. And different."

Keesha nodded. "You can say that again. That is one boy who marches to a different drummer." Jade raised her head, and Keesha quickly added, "Which is a good thing. He's not afraid of romance like most of the mouthbreathers at Wheaton High. I wish I had a boyfriend like him."

"What about Kip?" Jade asked, remembering the two of them on the dance floor at the Atomic Café. "You guys seemed to be really into each other."

Keesha rolled her eyes. "I'm so over him. One minute he's all 'You're the one for me,' and the next he's ignoring me in the halls."

"But what about your CAD class?" Jade asked. "I thought he was always saving you a seat."

"He can save all the seats he wants," Keesha retorted. "I'm outta that class. I changed my schedule yesterday. I'm back in Figure Drawing, where I belong."

Keesha circled the warehouse district several more times and then followed the access road by the freeway. But they found no sign of Adam—or of the seniors from Hyde Park—anywhere.

It finally grew too dark to see, and Jade told Keesha to drive her home. "They're not out here anymore. They've probably all gone back to Hyde Park Manor."

Keesha revved the VW's engine. "Then that's where you need to be." She whipped a U-turn in the middle of Calumet Avenue and pointed the car toward Hyde Park.

When they got to Hyde Park Manor they sat in the car and looked up at the big stone building. Lights shone from the windows in many of the apartments. They could see shapes of people moving around inside of a few.

Jade stared up at the imposing building. "I can't do it," she said in a tiny voice. "I can't bring myself to go in there and face Miss Perkins and Dolly and the others. Adam might be able to forgive me, but they never will."

Keesha dug in her bag for her cell phone and tossed it to Jade. "You know what to do."

Jade took the phone and stepped out of the car onto the grass in front of the Manor. She stared up at the windows of the third-floor apartment, where she knew Adam lived. The lights were on in both of the windows facing the street. Before she lost her nerve, she tapped in his number.

After three rings, someone answered. It was Adam.

Jade kicked into overdrive. "Adam, it's me, Jade. Please, don't hang up! I'm standing out in front of your building. Keesha told me about her conversation with you, and it's true about the letter going to the wrong person. But it turned out it wasn't the wrong person, it was the right person, only I didn't know it at first, but I know it now, and well . . . I'm sorry about the whole mess."

As she spoke, Jade could see someone moving in the third-floor apartment. Then, Adam, with the phone held to his ear, stepped up to the window and looked down at her.

"See?" she said to his silhouette in the window. "I'm here. To explain, and to tell you things aren't the way you think they are."

"I know that," Adam replied in a quiet voice. "Keesha told me."

"No, no, no!" Jade shook her head in big moves so he could see her. "Forget the letter. That's history. I'm sorry about that whole thing."

"I am too," Adam said. "Thanks for coming to apologize. I appreciate it."

The phone clicked off. Jade stood still, staring up at the window, listening to dead air. Adam watched her from the window for a few more seconds. Then he turned and walked away.

Jade's eyes blurred as tears sprang to her eyes. There was no way she could explain to him what had happened. It was hard enough for *her* to understand. For three years Zephyr had been the boy she had dreamed about. Then, Adam had come into her life and, in a heartbeat, her feelings had changed.

Jade stared up at the window, willing him to come back. But it didn't happen. Finally she gave up and got back in the car.

"It's over," she said in barely a whisper. "He'll never forgive me."

For once, Keesha was at a loss for words. She put the car in gear, and the two friends drove home in miserable silence.

13

Thursday was agony. Jade couldn't con-centrate on any of her classes at school. Every hour she fretted that she might run into Adam in the halls between periods, and then was disappointed when she didn't. By the end of the day she was worn out from worrying. That night, when she should have been rehearsing her songs for the Battle of the Bands, she restlessly paced the floor, waiting for the phone to ring.

Friday morning, Jade was so exhausted that she slept through her alarm. When she realized she only had five minutes to get dressed, eat breakfast, and get to school, she collapsed back on her bed, too overwhelmed to move.

Her mother knocked on her doorsill around noon. She carried a glass of orange juice in one hand and a cup of coffee in the other. "Are you gathering your strength for the big Battle of the Bands tonight?" Mrs. Chandler asked, sitting on the end of Jade's bed. "Or just playing hooky?"

Jade lay flat on her back and stared up at the ceiling. "I'm not sure what I'm doing," she mumbled. "I think I'm waiting for it to be over."

"For what to be over?" her mother asked, handing her the glass of juice.

"The whole awfulness with Adam," Jade replied. She held the juice glass but didn't take a drink. Instead, she kept staring at the ceiling. "How could things that were going so great go so bad?"

Her mother smoothed Jade's bangs away from her forehead and smiled down at her. "I ask myself that twenty times a day in the real estate business. But you wait, it'll suddenly flip back again and everything will be fine."

"Promise?" Jade raised her head off the pillow and took a sip of juice.

Her mother nodded. "Remember that

eyesore I've been complaining about on Erie Avenue? Well, I thought I'd be stuck with that hunk of metal and concrete forever. But, suddenly, things changed."

"Really?" Jade mumbled, trying to sound interested. Her mother could ramble on about real estate for hours.

"I got a call this morning from the owner, Mr. Mullins. He was so excited, he could barely talk," Mrs. Chandler explained, blowing on her hot cup of coffee. "It seems that those art vandals have painted a pretty wonderful picture on the side of the building."

Jade choked on her orange juice. "Do you mean Art Attack?" she said, coughing and dabbing at her mouth.

Mrs. Chandler snapped her fingers and pointed at Jade. "The very same. The *Tribune* sent a photographer out to the building, and we're already getting calls from interested buyers."

Jade pulled herself up to a sitting position. "Wow, that was fast! How long does it take to paint a mural?"

Her mother shrugged. "I'm not sure. With a group of people working with rollers and house paint, a few days, maybe—maybe even overnight. I guess it depends on the size of the picture. This one is painted to look like a building with a door that is slightly ajar. You get a glimpse of what's inside the building through the door."

Jade was all ears. "What do you see inside?" she asked.

"Not sure. I haven't seen it yet." Mrs. Chandler took another sip of coffee. "But I'm going to look at it later today. You should check it out. It's near your school, behind Signature Hill. They may still be working on it. Mr. Mullins said he thought he saw a few of the *artistes* carrying paint buckets near the building this morning."

"This morning?" That was all the encouragement Jade needed. She flung back the bedcovers and hopped out of bed. Her mind was racing. Maybe Adam was still there. Maybe she could really talk to him. Maybe, after a few days, he wasn't so mad at her. Maybe now he'd be willing to listen to her. Those were a lot of maybes.

"Whoa!" her mother said, laughing as she leaned back out of Jade's way. "That sure lit your fire!"

An hour later, Jade was on the street

heading for Erie Avenue. She would have been on her way sooner but she had taken the time to shower, put on makeup, and dress up in her outfit—the one she had worn on Wednesday afternoon, when Adam was a no-show.

As Jade came round the corner, she spotted a white-haired woman in blue shorts, white polo shirt, and a visor standing at attention down the street.

"Vivian!" Jade ducked behind the gas pump of a boarded-up filling station and considered her options. The retired army colonel was on lookout. That meant Art Attack was still working on the mural. Should Jade go ask Vivian if Adam was there? What if Vivian gave her the same chilly reception Adam's mother had given her on the phone? Jade didn't know if she could handle that.

She leaned forward to check out the street. Maybe she could follow the line of parked cars to the mural, staying out of sight behind them until she got close enough to make a run for the mural. But there weren't that many cars, which meant there were some pretty big open spaces in between them.

"I see you over there!" Vivian's voice boomed from across the street.

Jade jumped and flattened herself against the gas pump. She held her breath and tried not to make a sound.

"They may have given me the guard duty because I'm a lousy painter," Vivian continued. "But I take it seriously. And I'm pretty darn good at it."

Jade didn't know what to do: Stand up and pretend like she wasn't hiding? No. She was better off beating a hasty retreat.

She was about to bolt when Vivian called, "You could run away, but I've already seen you."

Jade stayed frozen in a crouched position. Finally she called meekly, "Is Adam there? I was hoping to see him. Even though he doesn't want to see me."

"No. The boy's gone home."

"Oh." Jade slowly got to her feet and looked at Vivian. "Then I guess I'll go too."

"You'll do no such thing," Vivian said, taking a wide stance and folding her arms across her chest like a drill sergeant. "Not until you've seen the mural."

"I'd like to see it," Jade said, inching her way out from behind the gas pump. "Adam is a wonderful artist. And person. Would you tell him that, please?" She looked down and said miserably, "He probably hates me too much to ever hear it from me."

Vivian didn't reply. She glanced over both shoulders to make sure no other sightseers had joined them, then barked, "Follow me."

Vivian led Jade down the street in a zigzag route to the warehouse. "Can't be too careful," she whispered hoarsely. "The public seems to like our pictures, but the cops may have a different opinion."

"Where are George and Dolly, and the rest of the gang?" Jade asked, looking around the streets.

"We put the finishing touches on today. They were just loading the van," Vivian said as they neared the building. Jade could smell the fresh paint in the air. "You came just in time," Vivian added. "Five minutes more and we'd have been gone."

Vivian continued to talk, but Jade wasn't paying attention. She was too busy staring at the mural. Her mother had been right: The building had been painted to look like an old barn. The barn door was standing ajar, revealing a glimpse of what was behind. And the scene painted behind the door took her breath away!

It was a detail of a forest scene. In the forest was a girl, sitting on a bench, just like the little statue behind the cottage on Bramble Lane. Another figure knelt in front of her. It was Snow White and Doc—only different versions of them. This Snow White had sparkling green eyes and magenta-colored hair, just like Jade's. The girl in the painting smiled sadly down at a dark-haired boy in a derby. There was absolute love beaming from his eyes as he gazed up at the beautiful girl.

"They say a picture is worth a thousand words," Vivian said quietly. "Now do you think Adam hates you?"

Jade couldn't talk. For the second time in a week, tears blurred her vision. She fluttered her hand in the air, trying to regain her composure. Then she asked, "Do you think I can borrow a brush and some paint?"

Vivian pointed to some paint supplies stacked in the shadow of the building, covered by a tarp. "Help yourself. But the picture is finished."

Jade nodded. "I know. But I have a message for Adam. And I need to write it in big bold letters so he'll believe me."

Vivian pushed her visor back off her forehead and studied Jade's face intently. "All right," she said at last. "I'll tell the others we're done here. And I'll leave you alone to write your message."

Jade knew exactly what she wanted to say. She opened a can of red paint, dipped a broad brush into it, and began her love letter to Adam.

It only took her fifteen minutes to write her message on a clear part of the wall. When she was done, Jade hid the paint can and brush back under the tarp. She paused to check her work one last time, and made a silent prayer that Adam would see it. The letters were big and flowery, but her message was clear:

Snow White Loves Doc

14

Jade waited by the phone all afternoon, hoping that Adam would see her note and call. But he didn't. The phone was silent.

She should have been thinking about the Battle of the Bands and the song she was going to play, but Jade couldn't concentrate. She was too upset. Everything with Adam was a big mess!

At ten minutes to eight, Jade's mother announced, "If you don't go to the concert now, you might as well not go at all, because you're going to miss your time slot."

As her mom drove her to the school, Jade tried to run over the lyrics to her song, but her mind kept returning to Adam. "I blew it," she moaned, slumping down in the passenger seat. "I totally blew it."

Mrs. Chandler, who was struggling to get Jade to Wheaton High without breaking every traffic rule in the book, ordered, "Forget about boys and concentrate on your music. Warm up! Hum!"

Humming helped her warm up her voice, but it couldn't make her mind stop thinking about Adam.

The Battle of the Bands was in full swing when Jade arrived at the Wheaton High School gymnasium. The Phreeze had already started playing and they were the band on the list ahead of her.

"Okay," she muttered as she set her guitar case on the floor and flipped it open. "Mom was right! I should have left earlier."

The boys in Side Effects were huddled in the hall outside the gym, listening as the Phreeze took the roof off the gym with their high-energy rock. Mac Holloway was beating his hands against the wall, echoing the drummer's staccato beat. Charlie Riddle was revved up, too, bobbing his head in time with the music. Zephyr spotted Jade and nodded a hello.

A stage manager in a wireless headset hurried up to Jade. She glanced down at the clipboard in her hand. "Jade Chandler? You're next!" she shouted over the music. "Are you ready?"

"I-I don't know," Jade stammered. She tried to hurry, but her hands were shaking uncontrollably. She looped her guitar strap over her shoulder and fumbled to attach it to her sparkle-red Telecaster.

The Phreeze concluded their song with a deafening power chord, and the kids in the gym went wild, shouting and whistling their approval.

"You're up!" the stage manager urged. "Come on, let's go."

"Oh, god!" Jade hadn't had a chance to tune her guitar, set her amplifier, or even take a breath. She wasn't going to make it. This was her big break, and she was blowing it. Knowing that only made her hands shake more.

The stage manager clutched her headset and spoke into her microphone. "She's not ready. I'm sending out Side Effects." She pointed to Zephyr. "You guys are on."

"No, wait!" Jade cried. "I can get it together, really."

After a quick consultation with his band, Zephyr hurried over to her and said, "Look, the offer still stands to join us. We'll go onstage and play one tune, then I'll introduce you. You can plug into my amp and do your song. We'll back you up."

Jade looked up at Zeph in amazement. "You'd do that for me? Why?"

Zephyr shrugged. "We want to win this contest. And with you in our band, the Phreeze won't have a chance."

"Somebody get on the stage, now!" the stage manager barked.

Jade touched Zephyr's arm. "Thanks for the generous offer. But I've got to give it a try—alone."

Jade grabbed her amplifier and followed the stage manager into the gymnasium. She tripped up the steps to the darkened stage and hurried toward the center mike.

Jade pressed her ear to her strings and quickly tried to tune her guitar as Mr. Cooper, the emcee, announced, "The next contestant is an awesome senior from Wheaton High: Ms. Jade Chandler. Strut your stuff!"

The glare of the spotlight hit Jade, and instantly her mind went blank. Her eyes swelled to two unblinking circles. A loud rushing sound of white noise roared in her ears. Jade had worked on her song for weeks, and now, when she was actually standing on the stage in front of the audience, her brain had turned to mush.

"Jade?" Mr. Cooper whispered from somewhere near the stairs. "Say something."

Jade shook her head, trying to clear her head. Her magenta shoulder-length hair flashed under the dazzling stagelights. She tentatively played the introduction to her song, but when she sang, her voice was barely audible.

"Somewhere in my heart I'm yearning,
Yearning to let you know.
Somewhere in my heart I'm burning,
Burning to just let go."

She started to sing the verse but struck a wrong chord. Jade flinched as if she'd been hit in the face, and stopped playing.

"S-sorry about that," she stammered into the mike. "I, um, wrote this song because I believe if you want something or someone, you've got to just go for it and shoot the moon." Jade's fingers fumbled to find the once-familiar chords that now seemed like a foreign language to her. "But I seem to have forgotten how to do that."

Suddenly music surged from the bank of speakers. Jade spun to see where it was coming from. There was Zephyr, standing behind her, playing the opening chords of her song on his guitar. Jade was confused. Did they want her to leave the stage? "What are you doing here?" she rasped.

"A friend of mine asked me to deliver a message to you," he whispered back.

"Now? Here?" Jade asked, flustered. "What friend?"

"Adam." Zephyr struck the next chord of her song. "He got your note. He wants you to know he's in the house and ready to run up and down the aisles, cheering."

"What?" Jade spun to face the crowd. Rows of teenagers stood silently watching the stage, waiting for something to happen.

A familiar voice from the back of the crowd cut through the silence. "Jade! Over here!"

Jade squinted into the darkness. Two figures were standing under the exit sign, waving their arms. Keesha and Lucy!

The girls parted to reveal a boy in a starched white shirt, black tie, and derby. He was smiling as he pressed his hands to his heart, then opened them out to Jade.

"Adam?" Jade's voice was barely a whisper. She turned back to Zephyr, who had been joined by Charlie on bass and Mac at the drums. They were all grinning. And, soon, Jade was too.

Suddenly Jade's mind was totally clear. She stepped back up to the microphone. "Did I get lucky, or what?" she joked, gesturing to the band. "Side Effects has decided to join forces with me tonight."

The crowd instantly sprang to life and roared their approval.

"We've got a message for all of you, and one special person in particular." Jade looked toward the back of the gymnasium right into Adam's eyes. "If you want something bad enough, just go for it. Shoot the moon!"

Jade nodded to Zephyr, who cued Mac. The drummer responded with an explosive intro on his drums, and Jade burst into full song:

"Take my hand, don't be afraid
To try and shoot the moon.
Don't listen to the ones who say
We want too much too soon.
They say that we're not ready,
They'll have to change their tune.
You 'n' me, we'll reach the stars,
We're going to shoot the moon."

Once the song began, Jade was aware of everything: the audience bobbing in time with her music; Mr. Cooper smiling and nodding; and even her mom, standing proudly by the stage door.

Jade tilted her head back. She could see Keesha and Lucy clutching each other's hands by the exit. Five new faces had joined theirs: Vivian and Dolly, George with his cane, and Miss Perkins and Alberto.

The one person who mattered most, Adam, had joined them. Jade sang her words to him.

"Shoot the moon, shoot the moon,
You and me, flying free,
We're going to shoot the moon!"

Zephyr and Charlie joined Jade in tight harmony on the last chorus. Jade finished the song with a crashing chord, and raised her arm high above her head. She was out of breath, and her face glistened with perspiration.

After a moment of silence, the gymnasium exploded with cheers. The whistles and shouts were deafening. It was unbelievable. Everywhere Jade looked, kids were jumping up and down, screaming.

Zephyr's voice sang out over the microphone: "One—more—time! Everybody!"

"Shoot the moon, shoot the moon!"

Now the audience was singing along with Zephyr and the band. Tears filled Jade's eyes as she unhooked her guitar and stepped to the edge of the stage. The night had been nearly perfect. Zephyr had proved to be a great friend and musician. Side Effects had helped lift her song to a remarkable place— they clearly had a future together. And the audience response was overwhelming. There was just one thing missing.

"Adam!" she shouted toward the handsome boy in the derby making his way to the front of the cheering crowd.

"Jade!" Adam opened his arms, and without hesitation, Jade dove from the stage into the crowd.

A sea of hands caught her and carried her to the one place she wanted to be: in Adam's arms.

Jade melted into his embrace, and tilted her lips up to meet his. Adam's kiss was soft and gentle. "Just as I thought," he murmured. "We're a perfect fit."

"More! More!" screamed the audience. Zephyr segued into "Big Trouble Ahead."

Adam brushed his lips along Jade's cheek and whispered in her ear, "I think you may have won."

"I know I have." Jade tilted the brim back on his derby and looked into his warm brown eyes. "I got you."